MAKE ME A MIRACLE

MAKE ME A MIRACLE

BY CHARLES TAZEWELL
ILLUSTRATED BY FRANK SOFO

NASHVILLE, TENNESSEE

Nashville, Tennessee
Copyright © 2000 by Hambleton-Hill Publishing, Inc.

Published by Celebrity Books
1501 County Hospital Road
Nashville, Tennessee 37218

Printed in the United States of America
ISBN 1-58029-108-2

Library of Congress Cataloging-in-Publication Data:

Tazewell, Charles.
    Make me a miracle / written by Charles Tazewell ; illustrated
by Frank Sofo.-- 1st ed.
        p.cm.
    ISBN 1-58029-108-2
    1. Christian fiction, American. 2. Heaven--Fiction. I. Title.

PS3570.A995 M35 2000
813'.54--dc21
                                                00-028188

To Two Miracles—
Louise and Praline

Proprietor, Proprietor,
* If it's no fuss—*
Make me a miracle just for us;
* Knead it full of blessings*
And please cross it with a 'T'
* Then stick it in the oven*
For Louisa and me.
—Paraphrase of Nursery Rhyme

—C.T.

To my mother for her love and support.

—F.S.

PROLOGUE

East of the last flaming sun—west of the final and loneliest shining star—lies a fair and wondrous land of milk and honey!

Some may call it Paradise.

But call it by any name or in any tongue, its vast and magnificent Celestial City stands serene and enduring a mere prayer-breath beyond that far and ultimate horizon!

It is more real than mankind's fondest hope.

It is more perfect than mankind's loveliest dream.

It is more eternal than mankind's stubborn abiding faith.

The first and perhaps the finest view of this great and far-famed metropolis is to be had by any newcomer arriving on one of the great incoming carriers.

As his fleet conveyance bursts through the thick dark barrier of morning mist, which lies forever on the rim of the universe where endless years begin, the traveler may see below him a breathtaking panorama of the Proprietor's incomparable Celestial City.

In the foreground, rising in all their golden and legendary glory, are the majestic Stairs—famous in song and story. It is quite obvious, even at first glance, that they were designed and built by a master craftsman. The width of their immaculate treads and the height of their polished risers could never tire the youngest or oldest legs.

This gleaming Staircase ascends to the ancient and impregnable Wall of Heaven which seems to lift to brush the sky. Guarding a wide opening in the great Wall are the much glorified Golden Gates.

They were hand-wrought and hung, so legend says, by the Proprietor Himself, long before the memory-time of any Celestial City inhabitant save old Shard, His personal chariot-driver.

Their purpose is merely decorative. They have neither lock nor latch. To encourage the very timid or fearful, they have always stood four cubits ajar—or the approximate width of a slightly obese elephant.

These much publicized Gates lead to the renowned Plaza of Eternity. This is a vast circle of winding walks and lush ever-greenery. Growing here is every variety of tree, bush, vine, and flower which the Proprietor has invented to clothe the small naked spheres which comprise His inestimable real estate holdings dotting infinite space.

The Plaza, lying just inside the towering Wall of Heaven, is the oldest part of the now immense Celestial City. It is embraced by wide and busy Eden Way. This famous thorough-fare is the pride of every Celestial City citizen.

On it stand the immense and majestic buildings which house the High Court of the Patriarch Prophets, the Board of Guardian and Trustful Angels, the Bureau of Recording Angels, the Museum of Great Antiquity, the Library of the Archangels, the High Command of the Avenging Angels, and the most efficient and never-sleeping Department of Celestial Transport.

Separating these mighty and towered monoliths—and with the beautiful Plaza of Eternity as their source—the broad and stately Avenues of Creation, Justice, Mercy, Compassion, and Adoration flow fan-wise like mighty rivers.

They cross innumerable happy-sounding byways—such as Halosmith Road, Cherub Trot Lane, Paradise Walk—and sweep past some thousand Millennium Circles to reach the far-flung and world-famous environs of Elysian Fields, Fiddler's Green, Kingdom Come, Happy Hunting Ground, Forest of Forever and Aye, Safe Corral, and Peaceful Reveille.

It is hard for the newcomer to believe that where this lovely Celestial City now stands there was once nothing but barren emptiness in the dark and infinite wilderness of silent space.

Then, according to the diary of old Shard, the Proprietor's chariot driver, and which may be seen carefully preserved under glass in the magnificent rotunda of the Library of the Archangels, the Proprietor came with a small sun for a lantern.

Shard did not write down in this volume of time-yellowed and fragile cloudskin how far the great chariot wheels had thundered to reach this particular place. It must have been a far piece of light years. His rocky fist had trembled when he wrote—"I worry over Awesome and Fearsome. Although these monstrous steeds can gallop for forever and a day and never tire, they are frothed with sweat from mane to tail and their enormous shoes which—when we began this journey had the weight and thickness of grindstone wheels for the shaping of comets—are now mist-thin from the length and hardships of our journey."

Shard then recorded his utter amazement when the Proprietor smiled and nodded His approval of this ugly, desolate nothingness. He shook his head in disbelief as he watched the Proprietor hammer four blazing stars into the black firmament to stand throughout eternity to mark the far boundaries of His domain. Then He spoke, saying—

"Friend Shard, here I shall build My great and glorious city which all shall seek and most shall find!"

The diary confesses that Shard accepted this grandiose pronouncement with a grain of salt. "Could it be" —his rock-hard fist worried the distressing question— "could it be that the Proprietor, wearied to exhaustion by their dreadful journey, spoke not in His usual omniscience but in the wild delirium of chariot fever?"

Shard's doubts disappear in the following pages and they express a growing admiration which is akin to hero worship.

"He can turn His hand to any task," he wrote. "Truly— should I live until the final tick of time—I shall never hope to see His equal as a jack of all miracles!"

Shard then covered an unknown number of eternal days with these scribbled entries:

"The final stone of the Wall of Heaven has been set in place and to look up at its height gives me a crick in my poor neck.

"He had poured the entrance Stairs. A magnificent job. I,

myself, would have chosen some other color than golden yellow, which is bound to show every heelmark.

"The Plaza of Eternity has been cleared and seeded. The Proprietor invented what He termed a 'rain cloud'—a dark blanket holding much moisture. When He wrung it out it irrigated the Plaza's many acres.

"The stables for His horses, Awesome and Fearsome, have this day been completed. As I write this, the huge beasts are contentedly munching their first meal from their mangers— which, to my eyes, seem as large as that star formation on His planning board which He has named the 'Little Dipper.'

"I am tuckered to my toes. I have been on call for six steady days and nights while the Proprietor labored to create the Earth and all the stuff which had to go around it. He didn't skimp on the landscaping. Every hill, valley, plain, and mountain has a nice variety of greenery. He provided it with the best utilities—a never-failing sun for light and heat. And a choice of water—brook and river fresh, ocean and sea salt— and warm or frozen storm-descending.

"The Proprietor calls this the 'Great Day.' He has instructed me to harness Awesome and Fearsome and to fetch a whole chariotload of earthly immigrants to the Celestial City. The Proprietor is delighted—but I, myself, am on the sorry-side. I have enjoyed our privacy—and we have been all alone save for a very nice young shepherd, by the name of Abel. His early and unscheduled arrival was the result of a violent argument with his brother, Cain.

"One could not ask for a finer citizen. The Proprietor, knowing the lad would not be happy on city streets, gave him a flock of sheep to tend on the fair Pastures of Eden. The songs he sometimes plays on his shepherd's pipe have fallen most pleasantly on my ears when I have taken my dusktime strolls in the peaceful beauty of the Plaza of Eternity.

"Now, however, with the arrival of a full chariotload of newcomers, I greatly fear we are on the verge of a tremendous population explosion. I am sad that this must be.

"After I drive out the Gates and turn earthward this morning, I shall pull up Awesome and Fearsome before entering the great bank of morning mist which lies forever on the rim of the universe.

"And I shall say to them— 'Look backward, my dear beloved beasts! Observe the glory of the city which the Proprietor, with our help, has brought into being!

"'As it now is, it will never again be. Each person, climbing those Stairs, will leave a grain of dust from the road he has traveled. Each one, entering those Gates, will bring all that he has learned and remembers best. The silence of its streets and avenues will be broken by laughter and by voices speaking in many tongues.

"'This is the First Day of The First Year of the Proprietor— and the Celestial City now belongs to everyone!'"

People came.

A mere trickle at first.

The confident ones rode in Shard's chariot.

The doubtful but wishful set out on foot and blazed a tortuous trail through the Valley of Death, the dread Desert of the Lost, and the formidable Black Crepe Foothills which led to the terrifying Requiem Mountains.

But they came.

In time, the trickle became a flood.

Swift, efficient carriers were created by the delighted Proprietor to replace Shard's chariot.

Today, one of these great transports may be seen arriving with its hundreds of passengers every minute from dawn to sunset of every heavenly day.

No one, save the Proprietor, knows the present population of the vast Celestial City. There are such oldtimers as Mr. Adam and Mrs. Eve Adam—and Captain and Mrs. Noah. There are such heaven-come-lately folk as Senor Sanchez of Tiajuana and Marion Smith of Perth Amboy who arrived on the four-fifteen flight just yesterday.

Nightfall of each heavenly day seems to draw one and all to the old Plaza of Eternity. It has a transcendent loveliness. As the centuries have passed, the ancient Wall has become overgrown with vine. When the Proprietor's many moons come aglow like votive candles, the vine's flowers—each no larger than a widow's mite—come out to pray and scent the air with a perfume that is sweeter than the vanished rose of Eden.

It is a most pleasant place to spend the time of evening and to warm one's ears by listening to some fantastic tale of the day's doings in the Proprietor's Celestial City.

Old Shard holds the firm belief that some of these stories might be pleasing to earthbound ears—weary of dissent, disaster, and destruction.

Here, then, are a few of the heaventime tales which have been told in the great Plaza of Eternity on some thousand or one night in paradise.

I

Otto Schnitter slouched in his seat—his usual self-confidence crushed by a feeling of unpopularity. He had been the last passenger to board the great carrier—now racing at full and excessive speed toward the Celestial City.

He had been a full two miles from Longfellow Consolidated when the plaguey thing had pulled up alongside his school bus and the driver had signaled him to stop and climb aboard.

Otto Schnitter had ignored the summons. A man can't leave a bus of kids by the side of the road. Even though he was having one of the worst attacks of indigestion he'd ever had, he'd kept right on driving to Longfellow Consolidated—getting the children to the doors right on time. After all, it was September 2 and the very first day of school for most.

Funny. For a minute there he'd never felt so doggone tired in his whole sixty-four years. His hand had been as heavy as an old bus tire when he had lifted it to turn off the ignition. He would never have made it aboard the carrier if it hadn't been for the young driver.

Nice youngster. Strong, too. With no effort at all, as though Otto had weighed no more than a skinny first-grader, he had picked him up in his arms and had carried him to this nice soft seat by one of the carrier's windows.

Ott was regretful that the kids had witnessed his weakness. He had built up an image of being a man of iron—one who could face and easily conquer snowdrift, mudhole, sleetslick, and washout with a few masterful twists of the steering wheel and his right Size 10 brogan doing the turkey trot between brake and accelerator.

"I'd like to leave a note," he had said to the driver of the carrier. "Somebody has to know that my bus is due for an oil change."

"I'm sorry, Mr. Schnitter," the driver had replied, "but we're already behind schedule because of your stubbornness. You have selfishly delayed and inconvenienced your several hundred fellow passengers. I suggest you think on that, Mr. Schnitter, while I levitate this carrier and endeavor to recapture lost time!"

So Ott, realizing that he was at the absolute bottom of any popularity poll, scrunched himself down in his seat and stared out the window.

On the surface of the glass was a dim reflection of himself.

The white curly thatch atop his Toby Jug face reminded him of a dandelion gone to seed. Beyond his reflected image, everything appeared a bit fuzzy. He removed his steel-rimmed spectacles to clean them—and found that for the first time in more than twenty years that he could see perfectly with his bare pupils.

It felt good—something like shucking one's shoes and letting one's toes rediscover such boyhood things as fields, carpeted fence-to-fence with bluegrass; country roads swathed in soft velvet dust; puddles of fresh, unchlorinated water bestowed for wading by a summer thunderstorm.

Mr. Schnitter, looking through the window, watched the earth become smaller and smaller. It reminded him of a day when he had been a freckle-face of six and going on seven. He had had a dime to spend at the county fair.

He had invested this great sum in a yellow balloon. A big, beautiful yellow balloon with a slow leak. Ott had watched it dwindle away just as the earth was now doing. It gave him the same empty feeling of long ago. He had spent his whole capital of days and what did he have to show for it?

"Hello, Mr. Schnitter."

Ott turned his head and beheld a motherly female, amply proportioned. She had a no-nonsense air which made him believe that she was quite capable of saying scat to a lion or shoo-shoo to a rampaging nightmare.

"How do, ma'am," responded Ott.

"My name is Seraphita. Guardian Angel, Grade 1. You've been one of my favorite clients."

"Oh, well—I hope I haven't been too much trouble, ma'am."

"Quite the contrary, Mr. Schnitter. You have been what we in the department call a Grade A, Wing-Over-Lightly Risk. Whenever you have wandered toward some precipice of disaster, all that was required was a tiny tug on your coat tail to direct you on a safe and sane detour."

"Thank you, ma'am."

"Before we conclude our pleasant association, Mr. Schnitter, can I perform any final service?"

"Yes'm, you can," said Ott. "As you know, I've always been kind of proud and independent. Never had much, but I've always paid my own way. I had maybe a dollar-fifty when I left home this morning and now it seems to be gone. I'm not accusing that young driver fellow of picking my pocket. It could have fallen out when he carried me aboard. Anyway, I'm flat broke. What am I going to do for walking-around money in this Celestial City?"

"You are a far piece from being a pauper, Mr. Schnitter. The Blessing is our monetary unit. If you will present yourself to one of the tellers at the Guardian and Trustful Angels—which you will find on Eden Way—you will discover that you are quite a wealthy man."

"How come that can be?" asked the amazed Ott.

"Regular deposits made by you through the years. Small things said and small things done. A kind word to heal. A warm hand to comfort. They do add up, Mr. Schnitter, in a most surprising manner. The children, too, paid in an enormous number of Blessings to be credited to your account. Years of children, Mr. Schnitter."

"They did?" Ott was perplexed. "How?"

"Every evening. At bedtime. They said—'Now I lay me

11

down to sleep. God bless Mama. God bless Papa. And God bless Mr. Otto.'"

"I never knew that. I never even dreamed it."

"Good-bye, Mr. Schnitter. It has been a pleasure and a privilege to know you."

"Thank you, ma'am."

Old Ott sat with his Toby Jug face cracked by an incredulous frown. Then he whispered to himself—

"They liked me. All those children, they really liked me. I guess some—a few, perhaps—might have loved me!"

His broad shoulders began to shake. At that moment, the carrier entered the great bank of morning mist on the rim of the universe. This was fortunate because it saved him from disgracing himself in front of all the other passengers.

In the darkness he could cry as hard as little Patsy Perkins had just yesterday when she had thrown up on the floor of his bus and had thought Mr. Otto might be mad at her.

His first impression of the Celestial City was favorable. People didn't push or crowd going up the Stairs. The mammoth Gates, set in the towering Wall, were even a more grand sight than he'd been led to believe. Mr. Peter, who had been named Portal Authority by the Proprietor, lived up to his long-established reputation for benignity—and his staff of young apprentices, working hard to graduate *cum laude* in sainthood, was efficient, impartial, and welcome-spoken.

It required but a few moments for Mr. Schnitter to have his soulprint checked with the one which had been placed in the master file on the day of his birth. He was then free to enter the vast Celestial City as a bona fide citizen and blessed with all rights and privileges.

Unlike most of his fellow immigrants, who are exceedingly anxious to ascertain their financial status at the Board of Guardian and Trustful Angels on busy Eden Way, old Ott turned right onto a broad and quiet path which wound its unhurried way across the Plaza of Eternity.

He filled his lungs with air which was sweet with the exhaled breath of flowers. He hadn't felt this limber and free for more years than he could remember. *If I was so-minded,* he thought, *I bet I could do a handspring.*

He had flexed his leg muscles and was about to try one when he heard voices and footsteps approaching around the next turning in the path.

In a moment a man and woman appeared at a goodly trot—as though Gabriel was about to give a trumpet recital and they wanted to get jump-seats in the front row.

Ott recognized them immediately. They were old and good friends, Charlie and Drusilla Klophaus. Charlie had once been the custodian of Longfellow Consolidated—and he and Drusey had had him for Thanksgiving and Christmas dinner more times than Ott could remember. He had been real broken up when the pair had gone away after a fatal vacation accident on the Jersey Pike. It gave him much pleasure to see that the Proprietor had patched them up and they were now hale, hearty, and chipmunk chipper.

"Otto!" cried Charlie Klophaus, rushing up with arms outstretched.

"Dear Mr. Schnitter!" said Drusilla—and then she did something she had never done before. She kissed him.

13

Otto had always thought of her as rather a plain women with a spare, New Englandish figure. As she drew away with a mist of tears in her eyes, he saw her as Charlie Klophaus must have seen her all through the years. She was beautiful.

And Charlie, too, had a different appearance. He wasn't a little bandy-legged fat man who had swept up the litter left by the kids at Longfellow Consolidated. He looked dignified and successful. Mr. Schnitter guessed that Charlie must have a pretty substantial account of blessings over at the Guardian and Trustful Angels.

"How you been?" asked Charlie.

"Tolerable, tolerable," said Ott. "A little strange at this moment. Like a kid on his first day of summer vacation—don't want to waste a minute of it, but don't know what to do for a start. I guess I'd better find myself a place to stay."

"You're coming home with us," announced Drusey. "We heard you were coming and I fixed up our spare bedroom."

"I don't want to be any trouble—"

"Trouble? Not a bit of it!" laughed Charlie. "I know you'd rather have a roof of your own—but you need some time to look around and find just what you fancy."

"It took us a whole two weeks to find this house of ours out at Beulah Meadows," said Drusilla. "But it was worth the search. It's as like the one we had back home as two peas out of the same pod. I've even got a big lilac bush by the kitchen steps. A most obliging bush. Doesn't rest from May to May. Any morning in the year I can wake up and say to myself— 'This would be a lovely day to see and smell lilacs.' When I open the kitchen door—there it stands like a big bouquet."

"Come on!" Charlie grabbed Ott's arm and they all started

down the path. "The man doesn't want to stand there listening to you yammer about your everblooming posies! Besides, I want to hear about Longfellow Consolidated! Are the halls as clean as I used to keep them? Bet they're not! I knew those floors like my own face. Why—some of those muddy spring days I near tuckered myself out..."

Staying with Charlie and Drusilla Klophaus was a pleasant time. They went sightseeing almost every day. Otto thought that one of the prettiest sights he'd ever seen was the great harbor of Fiddlers' Green where all the long-lost ships—with captains and crews—rode safely on quiet heavenlocked waters.

He was delighted with Happy Hunting Ground. The Indian drums and dances beat anything he'd ever heard or seen. He sat on a blanket and shared a pipe-of-peace with a Chief Munching Bear—and was invited to return in September when all the campfires would burn day and night so that their aromatic smoke would give the earth its hazy Indian summer.

The seemingly endless Forest of Forever and Aye too was a fascinating place. Charlie told him that the Proprietor had created it as a sanctuary for all His wild creatures. It had been given to them in perpetuity—safe from fire, gun, chainsaw, and bulldozer. They came upon a man with a parcel of lions who introduced himself as Androcles, formerly of Rome. Andy showed Otto the proper way to remove a thorn from a lion's paw while Ott sat cross-legged and cuddled a lamb.

And the Elysian Fields exceeded his expectations. Even granting that the Proprietor had such a green thumb that He could make a flower grow out of a crack in a slum sidewalk, His Elysian Fields were beautiful beyond belief. He had sown His seeds with a profligate hand—and newcomers, who had lived their lives in earthly cities, saw that loveliness akin to this might have lain buried under their acres of asphalt and concrete.

Beyond the Fields, rolling gently to an infinite horizon, were green pastures splattered pink and red and white with clover. They belonged to the diligent bees and the fat dairy herds. Filling comb and pail to overflowing, they kept the promise of the old prophets—that the Celestial City was and always would be a land of milk and honey.

This happy roaming-around time might have gone on indefinitely if Charlie and Drusey hadn't had a slight argument. Charlie swore that it had been chicken salad and Drusey was certain that it had been ham salad sandwiches which they had eaten when they first met at the volunteer fire department picnic.

"I'll go down to the Library of the Archangels and look it up!" said Charlie. "Did you know, Otto, that somewhere on the shelves everybody has a personal history book?"

"No, I didn't."

"Well, it's a fact! Every little thing that ever happened to a person—such as me almost swallowing my teething ring and getting a blister on my heel right in the middle of a Fourth of July parade. Would you like to come along and take a look-see at your book?"

"Some other day, Charlie. I think I'll just walk around and take in any sights I come to."

Otto Schnitter strolled slowly along the wide Avenue of Adoration. He examined the display in each shop window.

He leaned on fences and admired the garden plots in front of every dwelling.

Although outwardly serene, Otto was inwardly dissatisfied. He had always been a busy man. Even though he now possessed an eternity of time, his early upbringing had impressed it on his conscious and subconscious mind that it was a precious commodity not to be frivolously wasted.

There was a sidewalk vender at the corner of the avenue and Third Millennium Circle and Ott bought a milk-and-honey-on-a-stick. He followed the circle and came to the small park which embraces the Well of the Good Samaritan. He sat down on a bench to eat his sweetmeat. By moving his tongue very slowly he was able to lick away ten minutes of his time.

He twiddled his thumbs clockwise while he watched a cloud shaped like a school bus roll across a sky-blue highway. He figured that three hundred twiddles should take up another five minutes—and when he got to that number he went into reverse for counter-clockwise twiddling.

His thumbs slowed and became locked in boredom after a dozen revolutions. He rose from the bench and walked slowly along Third Millennium Circle. He envied each passer-by who seemed to be hurrying about some task or job or profession.

Steeped in gloom, Mr. Schnitter soon came upon a small cobbled way. It had a chancy, heaven-may-care air about it as it zigged for a few yards and then zagged out of sight. A sign on a starlamp post read "Street of Miracles."

The name wasn't new to Mr. Schnitter. Back through his years some people had mentioned it. Parson Dinwood for one, who had lived out his foggy senility in a resthome.

"You'll know it the moment you see it," the old man

quavered. "It twists and turns without rhyme or reason. Sometimes it even doubles back upon itself. But if you follow it faithfully—sooner or later you'll find your miracle!"

Ott had let the words trickle in one ear and leak out the other. He would have had to have a ton of salt to swallow such a fantastic tale. Still—here was the sign and under it was the most gone awry, grotesque, bandy-legged street he'd ever laid eyes on. Fair is fair—why not give it the chance of justifying earthly publicity?

Otto Schnitter faithfully followed every twist and turning. Small shops stood shoulder to shoulder and their windows were filled with oddments. One place, which seemed to be doing a brisk business, called itself "Bazaar of the Lovely Lost"—and just around the next turning was a cluttered store which boasted that it dealt exclusively in the most rare Impossibles.

He saw several articles on display—a jack-knife, a kite, a valentine—which might have belonged to him at one time, but Ott wasn't seeking some tangible souvenir of his past. What he wanted was something intangible which might brighten up his immediate future.

He was thorough. He followed every switchback and explored every cul-de-sac—but no miracle had popped up from between the cobbles or plopped down out of the sky to relieve his depression.

He had passed the old, weather-beaten building with its many annexes which is Number 10 and was approaching the corner where the Street of Miracles meets busy Eden Way, when he heard a door slam behind him.

Turning, Mr. Schnitter beheld a female person—her arms

folded pugnaciously—glaring at him from the porch of Number 10.

To be glared at by Mrs. Noah is a frightening experience if the glaree has not from long acquaintance learned that she and her spouse, Captain Noah, are two of the most pudding-hearted people in the whole Celestial City.

This worthy pair has always had the complete confidence of the Proprietor. Centuries ago, during a cataclysmic forty-day-and-night tempest, Captain Noah and his good wife successfully managed an astounding livestock rescue operation. Although the entire earth had been sogged-in, they had rode out the storm and hadn't lost an animal from aardvark to zebra.

The Noahs, therefore, were a natural choice for caretaking when the Proprietor had wished to provide a place for so-called dumb creatures to await the coming of their owners. And what better waiting-place could there be but the old Ark—its boards impregnated with all the familiar smells of furred and feathered ones? The Proprietor, for all His wisdom, couldn't think of a single one—and so Shard drove the great steeds, Awesome and Fearsome, down to a place called Ararat.

He had thrown a good hitch on the famous vessel and with a "Gee" and a "Haw" and a "Get-Along-My-Big-Beauties," had hauled it a zillion miles to its present location at Number 10 on the Street of Miracles.

"You, there, Otto Schnitter!" shouted Mrs. Noah in a voice which proved that the ark had had no need for a foghorn on its historic voyage of salvation. "Took your own sweet time getting here, didn't you? Not one tittle of thought for a friend with a pining heart!" She turned and called to the shadowy interior of the ark. "All right, Captain—you can turn him loose!"

There was a barking and whining and scrambling of toenails. Then, out of the ark's doorway whizzed a black-and-white comet with a frantic wagging tail. It leaped upon Otto Schnitter. It yipped. It yapped. It washed his old hands and seamed face with a warm pink tongue. It wiggled as though it were trying to shed its skin so that it could get that much closer to him.

"Spot?" said Ott. "No—No, you can't be Spot. I had a dog by that name when I was only knee-high to a butter churn. That was ages and ages ago. Just like you, he had an old skate strap for a collar—only he had his name on it—" Mr. Schnitter's fingers fumbled the strap and there, as clear and as readable as it had been on that long-gone summer afternoon when he had gouged it out with a sharp point of a tenpenny nail, was the word Spot.

"I can go right on taking care of him if you don't want him," called Mrs. Noah.

"I want him," said Ott. "I want him more than anything." And holding Spot to his breast as though the dog were a poultice for an aching heart, he hurried off down the Street of Miracles.

They had a fine romp in the Plaza. There was a goodly crowd enjoying its pleasant paths—and no one seemed to think it strange or ludicrous that a grown man and a small dog should display such obvious delight in a simple game of tag. In some eyes there was a touch of envy. They wished that they had had the foresight, in their girl or boyhood, to have a similar all-breed dog that would have been waiting for them at the famous Ark.

"Spot," said Mr. Schnitter, as they sat on a shaded bench to rest and recover their breaths, "we have a problem. I've been biding my days with Charlie and Drusilla Klophaus. Fine people. Drusey, however, is an arch enemy of dust and dirt. So remembering your idiosyncrasy of preferring to sleep under the covers both winter and summer, I think we'd best find ourselves a hole in heaven of our own. Come on—you lead the way and perhaps we'll see something we fancy."

They started along the vast circle of Eden Way and its great buildings. Spot barked at a group of young lawyers, each one still earth-damp behind the ears, that was running into the High Court of the Patriarch Prophets to hear Solomon deliver a legal opinion—and growled at the golden lions which guarded the steps of the Library of the Archangels.

They passed the stately Museum of Antiquity—threading their way through a chattering crowd of heaven-come-latelies on one of the many and popular guided tours of the Celestial City. Arriving at the wide and illustrious Avenue of Compassion, Spot halted and cupped his dog ears.

Some sound, much too faint and distant for Ott to hear, seemed to have an aural witchery. Spot turned and dogtrotted up the avenue with Mr. Schnitter heeling obediently as all owners have been taught to do by their more intelligent animals.

Third Millennium Circle was in sight when Ott heard and identified the sound.

"Children!" he said. "The voices of children!"

Then he knew that these voices were what he had been

missing—and why he had had an underlying feeling of lassitude and depression on his excursions to view the truly incredible sights of the Celestial City.

It had been as though he had been watching a TV program or a motion picture without any background music. For years, from September to June, he had driven his school bus to the incidental music of children's laughter, squeals, whoops, sneezes, yells, coughs, wails, hoots, sniffles, and general pandemonium. Ever since his arrival at the Gates, Mr. Schnitter's calloused eardrums had colored him bored because they had been missing the nourishing din of tots and toddlers.

Spot had led Ott to the remarkable playground which occupies the entire area between Third Millennium Circle and Christmas Eve Lane. In the center of this field for play are several enormous buildings, designed evidently by some architect who had majored in storybook castles.

Mr. Schnitter leaned on the fence. He had never seen so many children gathered together in one place—not even excluding the time he had driven the Longfellow Consolidated contingent to the county fair for Young Farmers of Tomorrow Day.

"It's a school," he said to Spot. "It's got to be a school of some kind and we got here just at recess time."

He watched a tall bearded man with a knapsack come out of one of the buildings and walk toward the fence—pausing at groups of children to speak and pat heads.

When he reached the gate, Otto spoke up:

"Excuse me. I'm Otto Schnitter and I used to drive a bus for Longfellow Consolidated. Could you tell me the name of this school?"

"Well—it's part school and part something else," smiled the man. "I think of it as an oasis for small wanderers. A caravansary where earth's runaways can crawl onto a lap and be mothered."

"Has it got a name to it?" asked Ott.

"You've never heard of Angels' Aide?" The man shook his head over such unbelievable ignorance. "It's been here forever as far as I know! It cares for all the children who come to the Gates ahead of their parents—and who have no close relatives in residence."

"Temporary orphans, you might say?"

"Exactly. It is staffed by an abundant bevy of plump, bosomy grandmothers—well-schooled in the art of the rocking chair, the bedtime tale, and the lullaby. Each one, I might add, has impeccable references from some other time and place for having overindulged and spoiled their own grandchildren."

"Must be a nice place to work," said Ott wistfully.

"I find it so. I'm their medical advisor. My office is just across the street and I'm on call day or night. I take it you like children?"

"We cotton to each other real good."

"You aren't unnerved by the hullabaloo they can cause at odd and unexpected moments for no apparent reason?"

"I'm used to it. I don't hardly hear it."

"Good!" beamed the bearded man. "You may be the answer to my problem. I have a small apartment for rent over my dispensary across the way. Prospective tenants have all said that it would be much too noisy—what with the children and the traffic on the Avenue of Compassion. But—since you tell me that your are din-deaf—"

"My dog and I would like to look at it," said Ott, and he and Spot and the man went across Compassion to a red brick building with small paned windows which displayed red and green apothecary jars. By the doorway was a hanging sign of modest size which read "Luke the Physician."

The apartment was all that any bachelor and unencumbered canine could ask—and that night Ott and Spot split a dream together under the same blanket.

In his dispensary down below, Doctor Luke slept with his knapsack of healing herbs and efficacious elixirs on the table beside his bed.

As usual, he came suddenly awake an hour before dawn. He listened and heard familiar footsteps coming up the Avenue of Compassion.

The footsteps stopped at the fence across the avenue. After a few minutes, they continued on their way and were lost in the silence of the sleeping Celestial City.

Luke smiled. Not once—in almost two thousand years of Luke's remembering—had the Proprietor's Son failed to pass by at this darkest hour of every night.

He had to make sure that every child was safe and secure at the cherub shelter called Angels' Aide.

Otto Schnitter took to spending his days at the fence of the playground. The children loved his tall yarns. Some of the littlest girls vied to make him the best mud pie. A lot of the boys begged the grandmothers for Mr. Schnitter haircuts. His constant leaning on the fence wearied the iron and the saintly Giles, of the Blacksmiths Guild, had to come out with his portable forge and reshape it.

A ball which had rolled or sailed into the busy Avenue of Compassion called for a set procedure. Ott stepped off the curb, lifted both arms over his head and bawled at the top of his bagpipe lungs, "School Ball Crossing! School Ball Crossing!"

When all traffic had come to a sudden and frozen halt, Spot bounded out to retrieve the errant sphere. To discover its hiding place was not an easy task because Spot—although of very mixed lineage—hadn't a single ballhound on his family tree.

His best fetch-and-carry time was just over five minutes. His worst was just under sixty. Traffic was frequently jam-packed from the Plaza of Eternity to Sixth Millennium Circle. Citizens waxed righteously wroth. They wrote letters and signed petitions. "Why?" they indignantly asked, "Why were Mr. Schnitter and his dog allowed to turn the great Avenue of Compassion into a needle's eye?"

He was told politely but firmly by the authorities that he and his canine companion must keep to their own side of the avenue and cease and desist from messing around Angels' Aide.

Ott took the reprimand very much to heart. Day after day he sat in the window of his upstairs apartment watching the children having a heavenly good time without him. Dr. Luke grew worried as he watched Ott's bounce evaporate and his spirits crumble.

"Why," he asked, "don't you revive some old hobby? What did you like to do when you were a boy?"

"I liked running a lemonade stand," glummed Ott. "Snowball fights. Halloween. Playing tag. Sliding down cellar doors. Swinging on gates. Climbing trees. Spitting through knothole contests. I don't think there's one that'd excite me to pick up again."

"No," Luke agreed. "Nothing else you can remember?"

"Oh, I used to go down to the depot every day to watch the 3:23 come in. Real exciting it was. Traveling men—drummers we called them—coming into town from New York—Boston—Chicago—sometimes even from Denver or San Francisco!"

"We have carriers arriving at the foot of the Stairs every few minutes. Traveling men, women, and children coming into the Celestial City from every place you ever heard of. Would it interest you to watch?"

"Might." Mr. Schnitter's head had lifted at the word 'children.' "Spot and me just might do that."

Within a week, Doctor Luke's lodgers were spending all their daylight hours outside the famous Gates. They took over the bottom Step of the gleaming Stairs.

"It's a disgrace!" Phut, Scheduler Chief of Carriers, complained bitterly to Gatekeeper Peter. "I had a bishop and a cardinal on Flight 92 yesterday. All their lives they had publicized the beauty and glory of the Celestial City! And what is their first view of it? A fat man and an old dog sharing a lunch out of a paper bag!"

"They're giving that step a nice luster with their posteriors," placated Mr. Peter. "Isn't this the Boston carrier just coming in?"

"It is. And it's thirty-four minutes late."

"Why?"

"It has a passenger who was about to lead a St. Patrick's Day Parade on a white horse. He refused to come without the animal!"

"So?"

"So we have a horse aboard!" snapped Phut. "Poor Mrs. Noah will have to take care of it until its owner finds a living place with a stable." He dug an elbow into Mr. Peter's ribs. "Now watch the busybody behavior of that Otto Schnitter."

Ott was at the carrier doors before they were opened. When the passengers appeared, he ignored the adults. It was the tot and the toddler—the sprig and the sprout—the pee-wee and the tadpole who were his sole concern.

And all the children seemed to gravitate toward Mr. Schnitter. They wiggled past their waiting Guardian Angels. They embraced his legs, hung on his coat, held tight to his hands and clamored for his personal attention—as though they recognized something dear and familiar about his square and sturdy figure. He was a rock of earth in a far unknown place.

Mr. Schnitter blew noses, smoothed cowlicks, hoisted stockings, buttoned blouses, tied laces, zippered slumbersuits, combed hair, and wiped sticky fingers. He was distributing honeypops when his eyes lit on the white horse.

Ott conferred with the owner of the horse. He placed five of the largest children astride the animal's back. Then—with a small fry in each arm and another riding his shoulders piggyback—Mr. Schnitter waddled up the famous Stairs to deliver this flight's catch to waiting relatives or a responsible grandmother from Angels' Aide.

"Look at him!" wailed Phut. "The Celestial City's centuries old image of the grandeur, splendor, and angelic decorum being Schnittered away! Oh, I do wish the Proprietor would catch him at it!"

"He's watching him right now," said Mr. Peter, looking up toward the heaven blue yonder. "The Proprietor is in the window of His cloudtop tower."

"I'll wager He's mad enough to cast thunderbolts!" crowed Phut. "Oh, that Ott is going to catch it! How angry does the Proprietor look—incendiary or annihilative?"

"He's laughing."

"Oh?" Phut's disappointment ran down his face. "Oh..."

Doggedly and mannedly, Spot and Mr. Schnitter carried out their self-made job of welcoming fledgling immigrants to the Celestial City. Every night they were near exhaustion. For six elderly legs, climbing and descending interminable stairs was an arduous exercise.

On a fine heavenly evening which, to be exact, was the eve of Groundhog Day down at Longfellow Consolidated, they limped into the Plaza of Eternity. Ott plopped himself down on a bench and took off his shoes.

He stared morosely at the peaceful scene. Strollers and sitters and talkers had come to the great park from every part of the vast city. Joktan, the lamplighter, came down the path with his small ladder on his shoulder. Around the starlamp which he had just kindled, some children were beginning a game of hide-and-go-seek.

Across the way, a brawny cometmonger was explaining a trick of his trade to a former steelworker from Pittsburgh. Near them, the inventor of the wheel and the inventor of the pin argued the importance to mankind of each one's discovery. Leaning against the trunk of an amaranthine tree was an esthetic young man in a robe of many colors—signifying that he was a bender of rainbows into perfect quarter and half circles. He was surrounded by a clutch of twittering females—student singers attending the renowned Academy of the Singing Winds and Whispering Trees.

"It's a shame!" growled Mr. Schnitter. "A downright sin and shame if you ask me!"

"I didn't but I shall," said the man who was seated on the far end of Ott's bench. "What do you find so distasteful?"

"The transportation arrangement for children!" snapped Otto. "What's the matter with the local PTA that it allows kids to be jumbled up higgledy-piggledy with grown-ups?"

"That's bad?" inquired his seatmate politely.

"Bad is a puny word to describe the situation. Youngsters should not be carried in those big, fancy, gadgetty conveyances! What is needed is a vehicle designed and made only for the use of kids!"

"Such as?"

"Such as a school bus," said Mr. Schnitter. "A yellow school bus like I drove at Longfellow Consolidated. When I picked up a child, I didn't arrive with a whoosh and all the power and glory of kingdom come. I drew up to a gate with a nice sweet stop and I tooted my horn. When I opened the door, a youngster climbed aboard with no fear at all. School bus yellow was the color of fun, friends, and a day's adventure."

"It must have been a glorious contraption," the man said wistfully. "When I was a child in the land of Shinar—which was a very long time ago—we didn't have one of those."

"Shinar must have been a very benighted place."

"Oh, no—!" In protest, the man slid along the bench to grasp Ott's arm. In the light from the starlamp, Ott could see a scraggy individual with moist blue eyes and a bird's nest of sun-bleached hair. "We were all well taught in the manual arts such as carpentry and masonry. My name, by the way, is Sek."

"Mine's Schnitter," said Ott, pumping Sek's hand.

"You know," laughed his seatmate in rather a zany manner, "I think it's our good fortune we met tonight!"

"How so?" asked Ott.

"I and my friends have been cudgeling our collective brains to conjure up a new project—" Sek giggled and clapped his hands— "and you come along and present us with a lovely and exciting one—a bool schuss!"

"A school bus," corrected Otto.

"A schoool buuus," repeated Sek carefully. "You must pardon the slip. I have an old affliction which sometimes plays tricks with my tongue."

"Hardly noticeable," comforted Ott.

"Thank you. Now, as I was about to say, there are many of us Shinar folk living near Sixth Millennium Circle and the Avenue of Justice. Furthermore, down in the basement of my own place, we have a very fine shop where we make and build all manner of things!"

"You don't say!" beamed Mr. Schnitter.

"Without a mumble, stumble, or jumble, too!" Sek said proudly. "Isn't that amazing? Oh, this is going to be a most happy and successful partnership! I make you this promise— if you will draw up the plans, I and my friends will bake you the mest bool schuss you ever saw!"

"I'll work all night and bring the plans to you the first thing in the morning."

"I'll see you on my corner!" Sek rose and started off down the path. "Goodnight to you, Mr. Schnitter! I must hurry home and prepare my pasement for our new broject!"

"Spot—" said Otto in an excited whisper, "I am probably

the luckiest man this side of Earth! That fellow has to be one of the careful, trained-from-childhood, foreign-speaking craftsmen a man only comes across once in a coon's age! Come along home—I've got a long night of hard work ahead of me!"

Dawn, heralded by the clip-clop horseshoe chorus of the milk-and-honey man's horses, found old Ott and his dog waiting impatiently at Sek's corner. It was a soft, heavenly morning.

An infant breeze, a mere whiffenpuff, toddled down the Avenue of Justice. It had been cradled on the Elysian Fields and it smelled of flowers and grasses. A sleepy mockingbird tried to imitate the call of a shepherd's pipe which it had just heard on the distant Pastures of Eden—calling all small lost sheep that had wondered afar in the night to come along safe to the fold.

As Ott waited and the minutes slipped by as swiftly as greased piglets, sleepers awoke and the Celestial City began a new day. The starlamps grew pale against a sky which had been washed and blued and spread to dry.

Spot gave a startled bark when a man with an exceedingly large nose threw open the shutters of the corner emporium. A banner across its front proclaimed that it was Ye Olde Aroma Bazaar—and Ott, studying a card in its window, learned that it dealt in every scent—exotic or ordinary—that any nose had ever sniffed onto any memory.

He stuck his head through the doorway to find if this grandiose statement could be true and there, on seemingly endless shelves, were thousands upon thousands of neatly labeled vials. He could make out the nearest ones and they read:

San Francisco Fog. New Orleans Coffee House. Virginia At Apple Blossom Time. Iowa State Fair. Pennsylvania Knockwurst And Sauerkraut. Painted Desert Dawn. Milking Time On A Cold Maine Morning. Young Girl Dressed For The Senior Prom.

Mr. Schnitter was so intrigued by the wares on display that he forgot to be angry when Sek galloped up late and breathless.

"So sorry-sorry-sorry!" he panted. "My jime got tiggled! Have you made the sketch?"

"Right here," said Ott proudly. "It's so clear a child can read it. Still—to be on the safe side—I'll come down to your shop—"

"No need! Absoldetwy unnecessary!" cried Sek. "For us Shinar folk, building a spool busk will be as easy as tweaking a goat's whisker!"

"Not a spool busk—it's a school bus."

"Right!" giggled Sek. "While we labor, why don't you and your canine hop down to the Bureau of Heavenly Transport and pick out a route for your elegant new schoob bush to travel?"

Bestowing a pat on Spot's behind and blowing a kiss to Mr. Schnitter, Sek of Shinar went skipping off up Sixth Millennium Circle and disappeared into the crowd.

Ott obtained explicit directions on how to reach the famous Bureau of Transport from the obliging owner of the shop of interesting aromas. The man was so nice about it— twisting his extra large nose to right and to left to describe each turning—that Otto felt he should make a purchase. For

Spot, he bought a vial of Red Rubber Ball Buried Underneath a Syringa Bush. For himself, one of Longfellow Consolidated School Bus.

The immensity of the towering edifice on Eden Way which is the headquarters of the greatest transport system in the Proprietor's universe made Mr. Schnitter feel microscopic. Making a quick estimate, he figured that a fellow would need seven foot legs, seven league boots, and seven months of Sundays to explore the acreage of its imposing lobby.

The entire floor was hand-laid tile of clear infinity blue—spattered and speckled with dots of brown and red and yellow and green. A plaque informed Mr. Schnitter that he was standing on a map of the infinite wilderness and its bits and pieces of real estate claimed by the Proprietor beyond the Celestial City.

It took Ott a long time to find the Earth. It was a very small dot on the vast floor of infinity blue. And such a far piece as a school bus rolled. A great doubt descended upon Mr. Schnitter.

He sat down and buried his face in his hands. With a load of kids, could he ever find the shortest, easiest, truest, and happiest way to the Celestial City?

Spot, as dogs have always done when a friend is in trouble, crawled into his lap and used his tongue like a pink eraser—trying to efface the lines and shadows of distress from Ott's Toby Jug countenance.

Mr. Schnitter looked down and saw a small black ant by his left foot. A mere speck of life which could be destroyed by the pressure of a fingertip. Yet half an ant lifetime ago it had set out from some far border of the vast map of infinity blue. Unlike

Ott, it could not see the sunlit Plaza of Eternity beyond the distant open doors—but it had all the faith, determination, and guts with which the Proprietor had endowed little black ants that it would surely get there.

Mr. Schnitter let the ant crawl onto his big hand. Rising, he walked over billions of major and minor stars and smoky galaxies—and out through the doors of the Bureau of Transport. He crossed Eden Way and put the ant down on a sunny sandy place in the Plaza of Eternity.

"You see how it's done?" he said proudly to his dog. "Transporting ants by hand or kids by school bus—there's just nothing to it!"

Since his unofficial job at the Stairs as self-appointed welcomer of children took all the daylit hours, Mr. Schnitter did his route planning after duskdown.

People wondered what he was up to when, evening after evening, they saw Ott and his dog vanish into the Bureau of Heavenly Transport. Ott's pockets were always stuffed with papers and he carried two starlanterns which he had purchased at the Sign of the Cybele Tub on the Street of Miracles from a Mr. Diogenes. Spot—for their midnight snack—lent a mouth and always toted a sack of hot-buttered ship biscuits from the Round the Horn Galley Bakery at Fiddlers' Green.

Mr. Christopher, Chairman of the Board of Transport and jocosely referred to as The Traveler by his close friends at the All Saints Club on First Millennium Circle, has always worked hard and late.

He had come upon many strange sights during his many years of journeying about—but he had never seen an elderly

*Otto Schnitter and his dog, Spot, plot a bus route from
the Celestial City to Earth.*

fat man inching his way along and using his dog as a mapmark.

"I beg that you forgive my unseemly curiosity," Mr. Christopher said to Ott after watching him for a fortnight of nights, "but what in creation are you doing?"

"I am picking out a route for my school bus," replied Mr. Schnitter. He then proceeded to give a detailed rundown on the whole project.

"Extraordinary!" Mr. Christopher was most enthusiastic. "I can help you because I've traveled earthward so many times that I know it as well as Shard knows the backs of the Proprietor's horses."

For many nights thereafter, he and Ott sat together on the vast floormap. Holding Spot on his lap, Mr. Christopher used the dog's tail to call attention to such route hazards as bogs of star-slush—the smoldering slagpiles of old, worn-out suns where the heat could charcoal a salamander—or where, if a turn to the right were missed, one might end in the far outer wilderness where the cold was so intense it would freeze-dry a polar bear in a milli-instant.

When the school bus route was down on paper and checked and rechecked for even the slightest mistake, Mr. Schnitter went out to Sixth Millennium Circle to find Sek and his Shinar craftsmen.

He found Sam of Schenectady.

And Saul of Sydney.

And Seth of Salem, Sid of Singapore, Sol of Samarkand, Stan of Savannah, Steve of Shiloh, Silas of Saginaw, and Sig of Swat.

But no Sek of Shinar.

Every morning and every evening, Spot and Otto searched the streets of the Celestial City. Ott pounded on so many doors he developed knocked knuckles. Spot smelled so many feet and footsteps he came down with a stiff sniff.

One night, tired and dispirited, they plodded homeward after another fruitless search. It was very late and only moon shadows occupied the streets.

To save steps, they took the path which crosses the small park holding the Well of the Good Samaritan. Ott pulled down on the wellsweep, worn satin-smooth by many hands. The ancient bucket of gopher wood, moss covered and leaking water at its seams, rose from some dark depth.

He filled his hat for Spot and then tilted the bucket and drank deeply. His Adams apple stopped in mid-bob when he felt a slight tug on his coat. Ott dropped the bucket and seized a hand which was exploring the pocket.

"What are you doing?" demanded Mr. Schnitter.

"I'm picking your pocket," said the pocket-picker sheepishly. "But, as you just felt, I've lost my touch and I'm not very good at it." He wagged his head. "As a matter of personal pride, I wish our paths had crossed at paschal time in Jerusalem a couple of thousand years back. Shorn of your purse, you'd have demanded of the Romans that Dysmas the thief be caught and crucified."

"Does the Proprietor know you're running loose in His Celestial City?" asked Ott. "And does He allow you to go about night-thieving?"

"Of course." Dysmas lifted his head and the light from a starlamp lit his dark, foxy visage. "Surprises you, doesn't it? I just happened to be at the wrong place at the right time. It was a black day in Calvary and I was one of the few who believed He might really be kin to the Proprietor.

"I took it with a grain of salt when He said 'Thou shalt be with me in My Father's place'—but danged if He didn't mean it! You should have seen old Shard's face when he drove down for the Son and learned that Dysmas the thief was to come along in the Proprietor's personal conveyance."

"It dumbfounds me," said Mr. Schnitter severely, "that you are allowed by the Angels of the Peace to continue and compound your criminal pursuits."

"We have an understanding." Dysmas breathed a regretful sigh. "During the night, I'm permitted to steal whatever I wish—from Aaron's rod to Mrs. Noah's arkmat—if I return it to its owner before sunrise."

"Tell me—" An idea kicked Mr. Schnitter in the head. "As a nocturnal prowler, do you know the Celestial City well?"

"I know every niche, hole, nook, and corner."

"Then perhaps you can help me. Do you know the whereabouts of Sek from Shinar?"

"I do. He lives on Babble Alley just off of Dilly-Dally Lane."

"Could you lead me there?"

"Nothing to it! Just follow me!"

Mr. Schnitter had difficulty complying with this cheerful invitation because keeping the thief in sight was much harder than tracking a black eel through a vat of ink. He avoided even the feeblest finger of light and flew from dark land to darker passageway.

"I swear, Spot," wheezed Ott, "the critter must rub his legs with slippery elm to run so slick!"

Several times they were left far behind and hopelessly lost. Then Spot's nose would find the trail and off they would go again at a heartpounding pace.

Skidding on the worn cobbles as they rounded a sharp and lightless corner, Ott was yanked to a halt by a hand on his coattails.

"Quiet!" hissed Dysmas' voice. "We go down this alley! On tiptoe! Don't awaken the smallest sound!"

Mr. Schnitter did his best to obey this command but his brogans, already incensed at being used as track shoes, now squeaked in protest at being cast as ballet slippers.

"Wait!" Ott whispered. He slipped off his brogans. "How far do we have to go?"

"Right down there," muttered Dysmas. "See that orange square? That's the window of Sek's basement workshop!"

The cobbles were cold and damp under Otto's socks as he padded to the window and knelt to look in. The scene popped his eyes and stopped his breath.

Never before had Ott seen so many people crowded into one small room. Every person held a tool of some kind in each hand which he waved and brandished without the slightest regard for any other person. Everyone was shouting and screaming as though it were five short minutes to Gabriel's trumpet time—and not one giving an ear to what a fellow worker might be saying!

Sek, making just as much noise and no more sense than his friends, was at the eye of this Shinar cyclone. Beside him was a lopsided monstrosity which had sails, runners, paddle wheels, propellers, oars, pedals, cranks, belts, clockwork, and other unidentifiable appliances and contrivances too strange to contemplate.

The whole outlandish contraption was held together by

bits of string, carpet tacks, safety pins, hooks, straps, tape, roofing nails, and library paste. It trembled under the slightest touch. It swayed at the smallest breath of air.

As Mr. Schnitter and Dysmas watched from the window, an adventuresome spider came down on its thread of silk from a rafter. As its feet touched the quaking superstructure, there was a terrible screech of tortured wood and metal. Unable to endure this new and outrageous weight, the whole incredible vehicle collasped and became a pile of ridiculous rubbish!

"What," asked Dysmas, "was that supposed to be?"

"A school bus," answered Ott in a stunned voice. "That pile of junk was supposed to be my school bus!"

"You're well rid of it." He helped Mr. Schnitter to his feet and assisted him down the dark alley. "It had only one thing in its favor. You could have left it anywhere and no one—not even I—would have stolen it. Here—," they had reached a main thoroughfare, "sit yourself down on the stoop of Jacob's Ladder Shop and I'll help you put on your shoes."

"Why did he do this to me?" cried Ott. "He seemed like such a nice honest person!"

"Oh, he is. Sek's one of the best. He and his Shinar friends are the kindest and most obliging folks I know."

"Then why—?"

"Mental block. Everyone knows about it. Goes back to their first project, the Tower of Babel. Very ambitious. It was to climb up to the Celestial City. Before they were even hill-high to a mountain, they went fuddle-tongued and never could finish it. It's been that way ever since. No matter what the project, they get to neighing and braying and it always ends up in a mess as bad as your school bus."

"I'm likely the only one in the whole place who didn't know that," said Otto Schnitter bitterly. "I should be stuffed for a fool and hung up in the Plaza of Eternity for all the smart folks to laugh at. I reckon they've been watching and waiting for me to get my comeuppance!"

"No, Mr. Schnitter!" Dysmas laid his hand on the bowed shoulders. "That's a Goliath-sized misstatement of fact!"

"From now on—," Ott rose to his feet, "I'll mind my own business and give no further cause for finger pointing and fun making. Thank you for your time and goodnight, Mr. Dysmas."

Then, tails dragging behind them, Otto Schnitter and Spot limped homeward through the silence of the Celestial City night...

In the days that followed, old Ott slid into the deepest decline ever witnessed heavenside of the Proprietor's limitless universe.

Dr. Luke, his landlord, was truly worried and trotted up and down the stairs a dozen times a day.

"I'm at my wit's end," said the beloved physician to Dysmas one daybreak when the good thief came to return the Aesculapian hitchingpost which he had stolen during the night. "He had been brought to bed by a particularly virulent and deadly attack of black disappointment—with a complication of erosive despair. His spirits have fallen down around his ankles like a suit of limp and faded red flannel underwear. Unless something is done to hoist them, I fear the worst."

"What is the worst?" asked Dysmas.

"I haven't the faintest idea." Luke sighed. "That's what worries me."

Ott had many visitors who came bearing gifts and good cheer.

Drusilla Klophaus brought great bunches of flowers from her everblooming lilac bush—and good old Charlie fetched him a music box, purchased at the Impossible Shop on the Street of Miracles, which at the push of a button played "Hail to Longfellow Consolidated School."

The redoubtable Mrs. Noah dropped in. She made it very plain that it wasn't a sick call. She had merely paused while passing to inquire after Spot's welfare. Before leaving, however, she placed a quart jar containing a dark liquid on Mr. Schnitter's bedside table. She gruffly explained that it was sassafras tea with a touch of catnip—a sure-fire escalator when cat boarders or Mr. Noah were feeling down in the dumps.

The children came from Angels' Aide across the avenue. The small boys brought him the treasures they had smuggled into the Celestial City. Such things as a Little League baseball cap, a length of fishline, a still good wad of chewing gum. Peter the Gate Keeper and his staff were notoriously myopic whenever they examined junior immigrants for contraband.

The little girls rubbed his head, patted his cheeks, held his hands, and breathed sweet nothings into his ears—each female tot trying her level best to give the fallen giant a small transfusion of love.

Thief Dysmas slipped up the stairs one night when it was wasting away to sunrise and slid into Ott's room. He dropped a good luck charm in Otto's hand—a horsehair ring.

"I braided it myself!" he said proudly. "While Shard was asleep, I stole two hairs from the manes of the Proprietor's huge steeds Awesome and Fearsome! Wear it and you'll be up and about in no time! Hair—as Samson and everyone knows—gives tremendous strength!"

But Mr. Schnitter's spirits were not lifted an ant's inch by all this loving attention. Indeed, they seemed to creep lower and lower as though they would ultimately ooze from his big toes and go underground forever. Then, on the third Tuesday after the first Monday after Epiphany, Parson Dinwood came to call.

Ott's old minister had been on his way to Halosmith Road to procure a halo for an elderly parishioner. Halos were long out of fashion—but all this lady's blameless life, she had dreamed of having one. Parson Dinwood could think of no heavenly reason why she shouldn't have a nice halo to wear when she sat in her garden on a Sunday evening.

Crossing the Plaza of Eternity, he had met Charlie and Drusilla Klophaus and they had told him of Ott's dreadful infirmity. Parson Dinwood had trotted off on lean shanks to pay a sick call.

This was not the senile octogenarian whom Ott had last seen bed-bound in an earthside rest home—the fragile ghost of a man who had quavered his firm belief in the Street of Miracles.

The present Parson Dinwood had had all his faculties recharged to the full limit of their capacity. He clattered up the stairs two steps at a leap. He came near to unhinging the door when he thrust it open. His grip, when he shook Ott's limp hand, said that here was a man who could throw a silver blessingpiece across the broad River Jordan with no effort at all.

"Old friend!" he cried. "What have they done to you? What has happened to bring you so low?"

While Ott told his sad story of the school bus, Parson Dinwood tramped up and down the room with great vigor. Spot sought safety from his pounding heels by crawling under Ott's bed. In his downstairs office, Dr. Luke could be heard scurrying about to rescue bottles which had been set to jumping about and even sent toppling from their shelves.

"Outrageous!" he roared when Ott finished. "Totally and abysmally outrageous! What is this place coming to that such an injustice could be allowed to take place? I say unto you, Mr. Schnitter— 'Take heart and gird up your spirits! I, Elihu Dinwood, D.D., am off to give the proper authorities fire and brimstone!'"

With that alarming promise, the old clergyman was off down the stairs. Traffic on the Avenue of Compassion was always heavy at this hour but the fire in his eyes and the granite of his visage parted the crowd for his passage as the Red Sea had once parted for Mr. Moses.

Reaching Eden Way and the great Plaza of Eternity, he bounded up the broad steps of the towering edifice which housed the Guardian and Trustful Angels. His old and angry hand was reaching for the doorknob of the Bureau of Internal Affairs when he stopped and shook his white head.

"No," he said. "When one has an important and legitimate complaint, one shouldn't deal with underlings!"

He marched out of the building and down Eden Way to the Library of Archangels. He entered the writing room—a favorite place for many who wish to send a love message by the midnight post of dreams to someone earthside.

Parson Dinwood selected a quiet table, a broad nibbed pen, a pot of the blackest ink, and an unblemished sheet of papyrus.

In a neat, Spencerian hand he wrote—

The Proprietor,
Cloudtop Tower,
Celestial City.

Exalted Sir —

When he had finished, Parson Dinwood purchased a ten-blessing stamp, affixed it with copious and righteous saliva, and dropped his letter in the postbox in the lobby.

Then, Otto Schnitter's trouble cared for, he hurried off toward Halosmith Road to resume the interrupted business of procuring a nice bright halo for his elderly lady parishioner...

The night had reached its prime and from the Gates to the far Elysian Fields the Celestial City slept.

Most people were in their beds dreaming of a heavenly tomorrow but here and there a starlamp still burned.

A window of the Ark was a yellow patch on the darkness of the Street of Miracles. Some pet had cried out in the night and Mrs. Noah was a very light sleeper.

A starlantern was a pinprick of light as it moved slowly across the Pastures of Eden. A small black sheep was missing from his flock and Abel could not close his eyes until it was found.

A candle still burned in Sek's basement workshop. He sat amid the ruins of what was to have been a school bus and wept bitterly.

The cobblestones of Eden Lane held a puddle of ochre which came from the open doors of the Stable. Dysmas, overcome by remorse, had come to confess the theft of the two hairs from the manes of the great steeds, Awesome and Fearsome.

"Forget it!" snapped the sleepy Shard, driver of the Proprietor's chariot. "They've got manes like waterfalls. Who's going to notice they've each lost a hair? If your Otto Schnitter gets any comfort from a horse-hair ring—let him keep it! Now take your silly self out of here and stop stealing my good night's rest!"

The Proprietor's Cloudtop Tower was still brightly lit. It had been a long wearisome day but there could be no rest until his desk was clear.

Petitions and prayers—a towering pile.

Peter the Gate Keeper's report on the day's admissions. Here of late he had made it up in what he termed 'saintly style.' All of the t's, dots over the i's, and the periods were illuminated Maltese crosses. Very pretty, but trying to even all-seeing eyes.

The star count.

The comet inventory. A newborn one, just out of its fiery crucible, was playfully chasing its tail and scaring the gravity out of the planets in the southwest corner of the northwest section of infinity. A matter of discipline which could be handled by Shadrach, Meshach, and Abednego and their fire chariot.

Captain Noah's account of pets received and pets reunited with their owners at the Ark on the Street of Miracles. Mrs. Noah's appended comments.

A letter marked "Personal" and "Rush" from Elihu

Dinwood, D.D.

The Proprietor opened it and read:

Exalted Sir—

I take my pen in hand to direct Your attention to what I believe to be a grave miscarriage of Your compassion and justice.

I ask You to search Your memory and to recall the time when Your earth was very new. According to the Book of Genesis, there was a land called Shinar. This was a dwelling place of a Mr. Sek and his fellow Shinarites.

One long ago day, they incurred Your great displeasure. In sudden anger, You punished them with a confusion of tongues.

I do not question Your divine right to a display of temper. You had suffered many disappointments with Your earth and may have wished You had never created it.

What I do deplore and cannot understand is the endless length of the dreadful punishment.

If man cannot communicate with his fellowman, he is suspended in a lonely, silent limbo.

If a man cannot be understood when he says "I wish to be your friend" or "I love you" or "Let us join hands and do great wonderful things together" what is there for him in heaven or on earth?

Trusting You will rectify this Shinar matter at Your earliest convenience, I remain Your humble and obedient guardian of Your flock.

Elihu Dinwood, D.D.

Sek was fast asleep in his bed beside his fat wife whose hips were as round as Shinar hillocks.

Suddenly his whole house—every board, beam, batten, and nailhead—began to glow and gleam as though it had been dipped in phosphorus.

He was awakened by a tintinnabulation which made the house vibrate from cellar to chimney top.

The scrub pails clanged. The dishes jangled. The kitchen pots chimed. The tumblers tinkled. The bedsprings twanged. The starlamps jingled. The silverware rang. The doorknocker bonged.

Sek knew that something tremendous was happening. He leaped from his bed and ran to the window. Leaning out, he learned that every Shinar house was as full of light and sound as was his own. Turning back, he shouted to his wife. "I love you I love you I love you I love you!"—each word was as clear and perfect as a drop of morning dew on a water lily!

In his nightcap and clothes he ran down the stairs—and he pulled down the street sign which read "Babble Alley" and tossed it in the trashcan—and he ran down the way pounding on doors and calling, "Come out, come out, Men of Shinar! Let us join hands and do great and wonderful things together! Let us build a school bus for Otto Schnitter!"

And they did. For six days and six nights they labored without rest. They created a beautiful school bus. A very motherly school bus. Broad hipped and big bosomed. They painted it a jolly pumpkin yellow. On its sides—in large block letters for any just-learning-to-read eyes—they printed "Celestial City Consolidated."

Puffing and straining, they pushed it down to Dr. Luke's dispensary. They got Otto Schnitter out of his bed and put him in the driver's seat. Then, putting their shoulders to its broad behind, they rolled it down the Avenue of Adoration, across the Plaza of Eternity and through the great Gates of the towering Wall of Heaven!

People came in from all parts of the vast Celestial City to see it. From Kingdom Come. From Beulah Meadows. From Canaan Common. From Jordan Shore and the Down of Promise.

Many—such as Joshua, David, Samson, Job, and Solomon, had never seen a school bus. Those of the latest generations of mankind touched a headlamp with a finger, ran a hand over a fender, or asked to sit for just a few minutes in one of the lap-soft seats and recapture their childhood.

Otto Schnitter pushed a button and the horn caroled "Here-Comes-The-School-Bus!" Everyone agreed it had more authority and spirit than the silver trumpets of the Heralding Angels.

The jubilant Ott took the driver's seat and put his big hands on the steering wheel.

"I think I'll take it for a trial run," he said to Sek of Shinar. "How do I make it go?"

"Go?" Sek scratched his head. "You mean move?"

"That's right." Ott was impatient. "What do I do to get it going?"

"I haven't the least idea," Sek answered sadly. "I haven't the smallest, slightest, minor, minimal idea!"

No one did.

The wonderful school bus sat in front of the great Gates of the impregnable Wall of Heaven as inert as a yellow pumpkin...

People refused to believe Otto Schnitter's grand idea

could come to such an inglorious end.

In the evenings, when they gathered in the Plaza of Eternity, whispers ran up and down the winding paths and stopped to gossip at every bench—

"Dysmas says that the College of Sages is working on the matter! All earthly knowledge is stored in their heads! They'll have that school bus rolling in no time!"

"Solomon the Wise is giving it his personal attention! Samson lifted the school bus so that the Judge could crawl underneath and examine the wheels!"

"The Artisan Guilds have been called into 'round-the-clock session by their saintly Patrons! All means of propulsion from the catapult to the rocket are under discussion! If they can't solve the problem, no one can!"

As the days went by the whispers, unwound by hope, slowed down and stopped.

Deprived of their comfort, people were forced to see and accept the immutable, unchangeable truth.

No one born of woman had ever made a vehicle that could travel from earth to the Celestial City and back again.

So had it always been and so would it always be...

The Celestial City seemed to lose some of its shine.

People were saddened to realize that even here there was a limit to the possible.

They complained that the clear cold water of the Well of the Good Samaritan had a sudden brackish taste.

Others grumbled about the growing dimness of the star-lamps which were supposed to light the streets and avenues.

A few even dared Mrs. Noah's wrath and grumbled about the night noises of the birds and animals at Captain Noah's ark.

On fine heavenly evenings when the Plaza of Eternity should have been crowded, there was plenty of sitting, standing, and walking room. There was little talk and less laughter.

The shops which lined the twisting, turning Street of Miracles took to closing their doors at sundown. Those who might have come seeking a heart's desire had been turned away by an ugly rumor. It said that all the shops were fresh out of miracles and that all the shopkeepers were cousins of Judas and dealt only in trash.

And day after day, the school bus sat before the great Gates of the impregnable Wall of Heaven as inert as a yellow pumpkin—because no one born of woman had ever made a vehicle that could travel from earth to the Celestial City and back again.....

In his dispensary below Otto Schnitter's apartment on the Avenue of Compassion, Luke the Physician slept with his knapsack of healing herbs and efficacious elixirs on the table beside his bed.

As usual, he came suddenly awake an hour before dawn. He listened and heard familiar footsteps coming up the avenue.

The footsteps stopped at the fence across the way. Not once—in almost two thousand years of Luke's remembering—had the Proprietor's Son failed to come by at this darkest hour of the night. He had to see for Himself that every child was safe and secure at the cherub shelter called Angels' Aide.

After a few moments, he again heard the footsteps. Luke's ears waited for them to fade away down the avenue. But tonight their sound, instead of diminishing, grew louder as they crossed the pavement and halted at the doorstep of his

*Luke the Physician finds a seed of inspiration on his doorstep,
left by a nighttime wanderer.*

dispensary. He waited—and then, as on all the previous nights, the footsteps went off down the Avenue of Compassion and the night was silent.

Dr. Luke got out of bed and lit the small starlantern which he carried on nightcalls. He opened his door and stepped out on the sidewalk. He held his lantern high but there was nothing strange to see. No mark or sign on the walk, the door, or windowsill.

Why had the footsteps stopped at his door?

Baffled, Luke turned to re-enter his dispensary. The swaying lantern lit the doorstep and he was momentarily annoyed to see that the surface, which he had carefully swept at sundown, was marred by a grain of sand or a bit of grit.

He was about to brush it away with his slippered foot but a sudden thought made him pause. He bent and looked closely at the minute speck.

A seed. A mustard seed.

Then the parable which the Son had spoken to His disciples in Herod's time and which had been set down by Matthew came to Luke's mind—

"The kingdom of heaven is like to a grain of mustard seed—which indeed is the least of all seeds; but when it is grown, it is the greatest among herbs, and becometh a tree, so that the birds of the air come and lodge in the branches thereof..."

Luke picked up the seed, laid it in his palm, and closed his fist upon it. The invincible power of the abiding faith held by that speck of matter made his arm tingle.

He looked down the silent Avenue of Compassion in the direction the footsteps had gone and he called softly, "Thank you, Sir."

Then, his starlantern banging against his hurrying legs, Luke the Beloved Physician ran up the stairs to wake Otto Schnitter...

The Celestial City Consolidated School Bus knows every road, lane, street, and highway.

It never arrives a minute too soon or a moment too late.

Rain, snow, sleet, or hail—weather doesn't bother Otto Schnitter's vehicle of pumpkin yellow.

Under its good hood is a single mustard seed—an engine of incredible and inestimable power. No larger than a mote of dust, it scorns the impossible and holds the firm conviction that in a bright hereafter it will lift and be a mighty tree where birds will nest and sing their loveliest songs. It has the go-power of the tides, the seasons, and the planning of the Proprietor.

There is always a crowd outside the great Gates to watch the arrival of the Celestial City Consolidated School Bus at the foot of the famous Stairs.

It never comes with a whoosh and all the might and glory of kingdom come. Mr. Schnitter frowns on such show-off driving. He is a master of the feather-soft stop.

When he leads his small passengers up the Stairs—a small fry in each arm and another riding his shoulders—the children are too intent on engaging Otto's personal attention to note that the Proprietor is always watching from His Cloudtop Tower.

Old Shard, the Proprietor's chariot driver, says the Proprietor doesn't mind at all.

Among the workers in His vineyard, He terms Mr.

Schnitter a specialist.

Otto gathers the smallest grapes and makes sure that not one is ever bruised or lost...

"Tell me," quavered Dysmas. "Did He by any chance notice Awesome's and Fearsome's manes?"

"Yes, He did," growled Shard. "I was driving Him in His chariot and suddenly—just as pleasant as milk and honey—He said 'I notice the steeds' manes are much thinner. To be exact, each one is missing a hair.'

"'Sir,' I said, 'There are times when Your faculty for being all-seeing is a pain in our long friendship.' Then I told Him about the ring you braided for Otto Schnitter."

"I wish—" Dysmas shivered and gnawed a thumbnail, "I wish you hadn't mentioned my name! Was He furious?"

"No," Shard shook his head. "The Proprietor turned very sad. He said 'Would that I could command such devotion and receive such a gift.'"

"He said that?"

"He did."

"Oh dear," said Dysmas. "I could cry."

The Patriarch Prophets, the Archangels, the Sages, and Solomon have always agreed that the Proprietor moves and speaks and acts in mysterious ways His wonders to perform.

Just yesterday He tossed them into an abyss of puzzlement from which not one could climb.

The Proprietor has all the wealth of His universe at His command.

Mountains of precious metals.

Acres of priceless gems.

55

Why—since this is so—does He now choose to wear—and upon His judgment finger—a ring not worth a widow's mite?

A ring such as one pauper might give another.

A common horsehair ring.

Made with a little love, labor, and larceny by Dysmas the Thief....?

II

Newcomers, viewing the beauty and grandeur of the Celestial City, are often surprised when they come upon the shabby establishment at Number 10 on the Street of Miracles.

The main building is of wood—the timbers roughly cut and hewn—and is completely dwarfed by a series of huge annexes which appear to have been added from time to time in a most eccentric and unorthodox manner.

It is a down-at-the-roof, crooked-at-the-beams, paint-bare inhabitance that should hang its head in shame as it stands there almost in the shadow of the majestic Bureau of Recording Angels and the High Court of the Patriarch Prophets.

On the contrary, there is a proud note in every creak of its

Old Cat belonged—Mrs. Noah was quite positive about that—and that was where Old Cat would be if Francis weren't such a powerful persuader!

Francis, formerly of Assisi, who has earned an enviable reputation as a protector of bird and beast, is entirely responsible for the two enormous carriers which wing forth each evening from the Celestial City.

The purpose of this flight is to cover the earth and search out every small creature that has been lovingly touched by a human hand and given a name. Francis finds them on a lap—or a hearthrug—or even a pillow—a trifle damp from someone's tears. Francis lifts each one gently and puts it aboard the first carrier. These will be reclaimed by the owner on some future day at Captain and Mrs. Noah's Ark.

The wild and the free—the fourfooted ones of the forest and field—the fish that swim and the birds that fly—every minute thing that crawls or hops or burrows, is gathered up and placed in the second carrier. They will live again in the peaceful Forest of Forever and Aye.

Old Cat had no intention of going anywhere. He was at his favorite garbage can, which was in an alley and behind a house that yielded a lovely type of refuse. Tonight, they had had chicken and the bones weren't even half gnawed clean.

He was a connoisseur of garbage—because that's what he'd eaten from the time he'd been weaned. He had never had an owner and had never felt the need for one. People were dangerous and sneaky. Whenever a lid was knocked off a garbage can, they appeared in a puff of wrath and yelled "Scat!"

And not one garbage can owner in the whole town had an ear for good music. Now and then he had seen a nice little tabby sitting in a window who had given him the yellow-eye and the tail-switch. That night, in a romantic mood, he had tried a little serenade on the back fence. But no matter how sweetly he had let the yowl come out, the humans had always scatted like crazy and had thrown anything they could get their silly hands on.

Satisfied with tonight's meal, Old Cat stretched and yawned. He had a very good opinion of himself. True, his black coat had a lot of scars—but they were like press clippings that could be shown to a female to impress her. And, instead of being combed and glossy, the fur was rough and dusty. He seldom, if ever, bathed. A tomcat should smell like a tomcat. Meeting a tabby, she'd know what he was and what was on his mind.

Old Cat sauntered down the alley. He had decided to bed down in a woodshed in the next block. As he came out on the sidewalk and started across the street, a car came speeding down the street. Old Cat froze in the glare of the headlamps—and the left front wheel caught him and threw him end over end into a lilac bush. He never moved again.

It was only a split cockcrow before dawn when Francis found him.

"Oh, you poor thing," whispered Francis. He bent and stroked the scarred and bony back. "You poor old thing!"

Then, because Francis is one of the kindest of the kind, he picked Old Cat up and took him to the Ark carrier. Many sleepers, awakened by a window rattle, may have thought it was merely the wind.

If they had looked, they might have seen a great shining

61

object winging over the rising sun and far beyond to bring the loved—and one who was unloved—to Captain and Mrs. Noah, at Number 10 on the Street of Miracles.

"Kitty?" coaxed the Captain. "Here, kitty—come, kitty— nice kitty!"

"Sssssssssst!" spat Old Cat from his tight sanctuary behind the Captain's desk. Coming to the Celestial City had been a shattering experience. He had opened his eyes to find himself in a flying warehouse that was stuffed to the roof with all kinds of animals. Dogs, cats, lambs, ponies, white mice, guinea pigs, hamsters, squirrels, monkeys, chipmunks, four skunks, and one small elephant.

Shelves, rising tier on tier, had held aquariums of tropical fish—and bowls of goldfish—and a quart Mason jar, labeled "Herbie," where a single guppy swam happily.

And birds. Everywhere there had been birds within easy paw-slash. Old Cat, the mighty hunter, had started to rise— and then had slumped back on his lean belly. For some strange reason, he had lost all interest in the sport. Indeed, the very thought of eating one of those bright fliers had given him a definite feeling of nausea. Old Cat feared, all his wandering years, that something like this would happen to him. The Scat People had trapped him in a garbage can and slammed down the lid. The Scat People were hauling him off to the city pound to be gassed. Sssssssssst on the Scat People! They'd soon find out that he wasn't a cat to go quietly.

"Kitty? Kitty-kitty-kitty!" Captain Noah sighed. "If we want him out, we'll have to move the desk."

"Nonsense!" said Mrs. Noah. "He's a tom and all that kitty-kitty stuff likely insults him." She turned to Francis.

"What's his name?"

"He hasn't got a name."

"Hasn't got a name!" cried the astounded lady. "You mean his owner never even—"

"He never had an owner."

"Oh, now, Francis—," the Captain wagged his head reprovingly, "you shouldn't have brought him here! You take him right along out to the Forest."

"He's a city cat and he'd be most unhappy out there." Francis gave a sigh that would crack a cast iron heart. "I don't suppose either of you could sleep nights knowing that such an old cat was so woefully miserable."

"I'd sleep sound as a sphinx—," snapped Mrs. Noah, "because I'd know I wasn't stuck with something that would never be called for! Do you realize I'll have him under my feet for all eternity?"

"It'll seem like only an instant," smiled Francis. "You wait and see—you'll grow so fond of Old Cat that you couldn't keep the Ark without him." Then, turning about, he was off before either of the two harassed caretakers could pursue the argument.

"Sodom and Gomorrah!" muttered Mrs. Noah. These were the worst five and eight letter words she could utter. "Double Sodom and Gomorrah—and I don't care who hears me!" She picked up a basket and lined it with a piece of blanket. "And let me tell you this, Mr. Noah—that cat is entirely your responsibility!" She placed the basket by the desk corner. "Don't expect me to cater to him!" She tilted a pitcher and milk dropped into a bowl. "You can put up with his ins and outs and you can feed the ugly creature!" She put the brimming bowl by the basket. "You hear me—the less I see of that cat the better!" Her back rigid, Mrs. Noah went to the door and then turned about. "May I suggest for once that you don't go stamping about and clearing your throat the way you do? Far be it from me to interfere with your pleasure, but the cat might like a lap of milk and a little nap!" She flounced out and up the stairs.

Reassured by deep silence, Old Cat risked one eye around the desk corner. A bowl of milk. He'd never before had his own personal bowl of milk. And a basket-and-blanket. This, too, must be his private property.

Old Cat, the carefree tramp, who had never owned anything of value, was both proud and worried by this sudden and meteoric rise to the bourgeois class. Ownership was a frightening obligation with a thieving vagrant prowling every alley. He oozed from his hiding place and crouched over the bowl. The milk could be protected by locking it up in his stomach. While his tongue stitched the white surface as fast as a sewing machine needle, he glared malevolently at his basket-and-blanket—daring any and all no-good vagabonds to sneak up and steal squatter's rights.

Eternal day became eternal weeks and Old Cat became well acquainted with the Ark and the Celestial City. His ins and outs were erratic and nocturnal—and Captain Noah, in order to obtain some semblance of a good night's sleep, was forced to give him his own means of exit and entrance.

In the daytime, this aperture was pointed out to sightseers as "The Dove Window"—the very opening through which the small white bird had flown after the Great Flood and returned with the olive leaf. At night, Mrs. Noah caustically referred to it as the "Old Cat Hole"—and never failed to ask the Captain if he was sure he'd left it open before she closed her eyes and prayed she wouldn't dream of the pesky creature.

Old Cat roamed far and wide on those heavenly nights. Finding no garbage cans was a great disappointment. Not one lovely smelling container in this city which was a million times larger than the one he'd known.

But there was The Stables. He came upon them an easy saunter down Eden Way. They were warm and smelled of horses and trampled straw and freshcut hay. Old Cat didn't know it—and wouldn't have cared if he had—but The Stables had been there long before there had been cats on the place called Earth.

At that time, they had been filled with tumult and commotion. At all hours, the huge chariots had rocketed in and out of the doors—massive wheels rolling thunder and the hooves of their fearsome steeds striking lightning. But now those wonderful, exciting, sweating days of creation were long gone. The great chariots stood idle and monstrous steeds had grown fat and lazy.

Old Cat leaped up on the feedbox for a closer look at the giant horse named Genesis. The enormous nostrils, each as large as a millstone, flared in amazement at this intrusion. Then the mighty bellows in the ponderous chest sent forth such a blast of air that Old Cat was sent sailing across The Stables like a tornado victim. Old Cat was impressed by this demonstration of lung power but not one whit intimidated.

"Sssssssssst!" he spat. Refusing to strike his erect and defiant tail even half an inch, he walked slowly and majestically out— each foot carefully set down to avoid contamination from this crummy place.

One memorable celestial night, Old Cat discovered the renowned Amphitheater of Harmony whose splendor awes many a newcomer when he suddenly comes upon it at the Avenue of Justice and Second Millennium Circle. Every day, thousands of music lovers crowd its vast and tiered auditorium to sit enthralled as they listen to the supernal melodies of the spheres.

The immortal Hark, old as the first enchanting sounded note, is the organist. Hair as white as a just-born cloudlet and face as heavily lined as one of his many sheets of music, he is the sole master of the mighty instrument—with a voice so great it can easily reach the farthest planet in infinite space.

Long, long aeons ago—and centuries upon centuries before there was anyone anywhere, the Proprietor made His galaxies— large, medium and small—and set them in motion. Each star and planet in every galaxy, He dressed in a different way—and like dancers, they spun and glided around His universe in a manner that was most merry and pleasing to His eye.

Each galaxy danced in the rhythm the Proprietor had given it. Some revolved to the idyllic simplicity of a pastoral; others twirled to a gay, whimsical caprice; many wheeled to a dreamy and pensive nocturne.

But, as the centuries ticked away on eternity's faceless clock, some of the big, corpulent dancers became a trifle tired and out of breath. Some of the smallest forgot their melody— and they made up doggerels and went skipping and hopping and playing hide-and-go-seek like children at a kindergarten party.

To remedy this, the Proprietor constructed the mammoth

organ and housed it in the Amphitheater of Harmony. Astride Balsam's donkey, it would require half a day to circle the largest of the pipes—and the smallest is no larger around than a mustard seed and so scant of height that Picklepuss the turtle could easily crawl over it and merely feel a slight tickle on his stomach.

Each celestial day, obeying the flying hands of organ-master Hark, it has lifted its powerful voice and sent forth uncounted glorious melodies. The far galaxies always hear and listen. Then, without a stumble or hesitation, they continue the whirling and gliding of their assigned dance.

Old Cat circled the Amphitheater of Harmony and carefully examined every closed and locked door. This situation was a direct challenge to his ingenuity and Old Cat accepted it with alacrity. Using his stiletto-sharp claws and best over-the-fence leaps, he made a perilous ascent to the roof. There, as his mind had pictured it, was an open skylight.

Peering into the darkness, Old Cat saw what he thought was a large tree. He had climbed up and down trees ever since he was a kitten. He took a flying leap and grasped it with all four feet. It wasn't a tree, however, it was an organ pipe—and its polished surface offered no hold at all for his frantic claws. With a horrified yowl, Old Cat slid downward at an ever increasing rate of speed and landed with a resounding thud on his tailpiece.

Old Cat rose on irate legs and spat at the organ pipe. A bump and a bounce such as that one could really ruin a rear appendage—and he was a very tail-proud cat. There was a long mirror above the console of the organ and a dim, flickering star candle left burning in the sconce. Old Cat decided he'd best examine his tail in the mirror.

He put one paw on the keyboard—and instantly a clear, sweet musical note filled the Amphitheater. Old Cat hastily lifted his paw and froze. There was such a complete silence he could hear his eyes roll. This was a strange thing he'd come upon. Interesting, too. Crouching low, he moved to the lower end of the keyboard and risked a paw on the last key. The resulting thunder shook every bone in his body.

Old Cat shook himself and then stole up to the other end of this loudmouthed monster and laid a paw on the last key. A pipe answered in a note so high and shrill that it made his teeth ache. Very interesting. He sat down on the bench and waved his tail slowly and gracefully to keep the meditation juices flowing freely. With the proper thinking, this might turn into a real fun thing.

He overturned the whole basket of thought keepsakes in his memory attic and examined every time-tested relic: those gained from experience, those cuffed into his head by his mother—and instinct treasures he had inherited from distant and unknown relatives who had yowled in the alleyways of Babylon and stolen scraps of meat from the animal pens in Nero's coliseum.

In the latter, he found the perfect idea. He laid his ears flat, opened his jaws in a frightful snarl and with a flying leap, sat down on the bass keys.

Looking in the mirror, he almost scared himself. He looked like a ravening king of the jungle and the thundering plaything made it appear that he had the full-throated roar of ten million lions!

He galloped up to the other end, fixed his ears, whiskers

Old Cat prowls along the keys of the organ in the
Amphitheatre of Harmony.

and mouth in a more horrible grimace and sat down on those keys. This was even better! He was now a bloodthirsty tiger racing into the arena to devour his hapless prey—and the plaything gave him the earsplitting scream of ten million tigers!

It was hard to decide which character was best—so Old Cat trotted back and forth, sitting on the roar end and then on the scream end. The Celestial City—and indeed all the universe—shook and vibrated. From the Great Wall to the far-out environs, people were tossed from their beds and came running into the streets in their night clothes and caps to ask what was happening.

The night watch of the Angels of the Peace, with wrath in their collective eyes, rushed to the Amphitheater—but Old Cat ran through the forest of legs and down Second Millennium Circle and claimed sanctuary in the Church of the Loving Heart. For further security, he climbed the bell rope. This woke the sleeping bell in the tower—and it tolled for thirty clangorous minutes before the night watch could loosen Old Cat's determined claws.

Even wrapped in a cloak for safety, it took ten claw-fearful night watchmen to carry Old Cat to Captain Noah's Ark. Every step of the way, he spat and yowled—and screamed to anyone who might care to listen—that they were wrenching his liver, breaking his back, and tearing his gallbladder out by the roots! He was dumped into a stout cage and left to repent his sins.

Old Cat wasted no time on repenting. He made a muff of his front legs and began to make plans for the day they'd let him out of the cage. It would have to be really mean. Maybe there was some good idea way back in his brain that had come down to him from an ancestor who'd been around during the Spanish Inquisition.

Miss Angela Barnworth, who lived alone out in Canaan Common, had been awakened by Old Cat's performance at the console of the mighty organ. In her interrupted dream, she had been back in her efficiency apartment in Dothan, Illinois on the night of the big fire in the south end of town when the gas tank had blown up. The dream had been so real that she jumped out of bed and ran to the window and looked out. There had been no glow in the sky and after a few minutes, the explosions had ceased and the bell had started to toll. She had decided it must be a very small conflagration and the volunteer firefighters were being summoned.

It was such a heavenly night—the air so soft and the moonlight so mellow—that Miss Barnworth slipped into a robe and went out on her porch to sit in her rocker and watch the fireflies pretend they were stars.

It was a lovely house—and exactly like the one she had seen in a magazine. She had admired the picture so much that she had thumbtacked the page to the wall over the sink back in the Dothan apartment. While she washed the dishes after a lonely meal, she had often imagined herself living in a wonderful cottage that comfortably smoked its chimney, with a white fence, flagstone walk, and snowball bushes that sat well back from the hustle and bustle of the street.

Miss Angela Barnworth was a comparative newcomer to Celestial City. She had been secretary to the third vice-president of the Farmers and Livestock Growers Insurance Company—

and her twenty year employment by that firm had been ended by a bus accident while she had been on her way to her annual vacation at a Michigan lake.

Miss Barnworth had come up on one of the late afternoon flights—although her carrier had been delayed for half an hour because Otto Schnitter was disembarking children from his school bus at the landing area for the Stairs.

She had been met and welcomed by her Guardian Angel Dodanim. She had liked him immediately—and was most grateful for his assistance past and present—although she could now see clearly why it was that no romances had been thrown her way. Dodanim was so old that he believed good guardianship for any female consisted of good health, a good job, and a television set.

Dodanim had taken her out to Canaan Common—and when Miss Barnworth had seen this particular house, there was no need to look further. She had made out a withdrawal slip on her account at the Recording Angels—a modest sum of blessings that used up merely a hundredth of a eulogy said by the third vice-president at a service for her down on earth. Miss Barnworth had found her dream house in Canaan Common—and tonight, as she rocked on her porch, she was perfectly happy.

Well—not *perfectly* happy.

Miss Barnworth had always wanted a cat—and throughout her professional life, it had always been her misfortune to live in rooms or bachelor-girl apartments where joint tenancy with a pet was strictly forbidden. She and this lovely house needed a cat—but how and where to find one was a perplexing problem.

A movement by a snowball bush caught her eye.

"Who's there?" she called sharply.

"Oh, plague it!" said a disappointed voice. A dejected figure appeared. "You weren't supposed to see me. It spoils all the fun."

"Who are you and what are you doing?" demanded Miss Barnworth.

"I'm Dysmas," was the proud answer. "I was stealing one of your flowers."

"That is the height of foolishness," said Angela Barnworth. "No one steals flowers here—they're free for the picking."

"I know," sighed Dysmas. "It's that way with almost anything. It's very difficult being a thief in the Celestial City."

"Tell me—," Miss Barnworth rocked thoughtfully, "did you ever steal a cat?"

"Oh, my, no! Francis wouldn't like it and the Proprietor wouldn't like it and they'd make me return it immediately!"

"I see." Angela Barnworth rocked some more. "Then how would one go about procuring such a cat in a legitimate and proper manner?"

"Well—," Dysmas said thoughtfully, "that's a tough one. I most certainly wouldn't go to Sek of Shinar. Ten to one, he and his friends would go right down in his workshop and start to make one."

"I don't want a made cat," Miss Barnworth was most positive. "I want a real, live, genuine animal."

"In my opinion, which is pretty reliable on the whole, your best bet would be the Ark."

"The Ark?" inquired Angela Barnworth.

"Number 10, on the Street of Miracles. You can't miss it.

It's full of all kinds of animals. Ask for Captain Noah."

"Thank you. Thank you, Mr. Dysmas."

"No trouble at all. Well—I must be on my way." He laughed softly. "Do you know what I'm going to do now? I'm going down to Luke's dispensary and pretend—only pretend, mind you—that I'm stealing his mortar and pestle!"

"Goodnight, Mr. Dysmas," Miss Barnworth called to his retreating back. "Have fun!"

She pushed her rocker to and fro with toes that had a delicious tingle. She was going to have a cat. It might be an angora or Persian. Or a Maltese or a Manx. Or just a plain, ordinary, purring and loving puss. A good-company cat. She smiled as she saw, in her mind's eye, this innocent, fluffy friend playing with her ball of yarn when she knitted—and the small, round depression on her bed where the sweet, trusting creature slept every night in reach of her hand. And speaking of bed, she must get there immediately! She must be up first thing tomorrow morning to arrive at the Ark when the doors were opened.

"No—," Captain Noah's white hair looked like a halo in the early sunlight. "I'm real sorry, Miss Barnworth, but we don't have a spare cat. All our boarders belong to somebody and are just waiting to be called for."

"I see. I just didn't understand." Miss Barnworth blew her nose. "I'm sorry to seem so emotional—but I was counting so much on finding one. I—well, I'm very fond of cats."

"I understand, ma'am." The Captain shook his head. "I'm ashamed I can't help you."

"Is there a chance—," asked Angela, "even the remotest

chance—that some time in the future you might accidentally have any kind of an extra cat?"

"We've got one right now!" said Mrs. Noah in a loud voice from the next room. She stamped in and, with arms akimbo, glared at the Captain. "He's extra and anybody who wants him is welcome to him!"

"Now, Mother—," chided the Captain.

"Oh, I'm so glad!" cried Miss Barnworth. "What's he like?"

"Black," snapped Mrs. Noah. "Black as sin."

"Beautiful!" sighed Angela. "Don't you think black is a truly beautiful color?"

"He might be that color clear through to his innards," Mrs. Noah replied grimly. "Do you want to see him?"

"Oh, yes!"

"Just follow me!" She marched off with Miss Barnworth following eagerly at her heels. "If I were you—," she admonished, "I wouldn't put my finger through the bars and try to pet him. You might scrape your finger on a hidden nail and mistakenly think the cat clawed you. Here we are!" She stood before Old Cat's cage and eyed Miss Barnworth doubtfully. "What do you think of him?"

"Adorable!" Miss Barnworth whispered. "Simply adorable!"

"Well—that word would hardly ever occur to me in describing him," said Mrs. Noah, "but then, he and I have never been what you'd call close."

Old Cat peeled back his lips in his most ferocious snarl.

"Look! Oh, look, Mrs. Noah!" laughed Angela. "He's smiling at us!"

"He does that a lot." She drew back a step. "Ever since he came here, he's been smiling like that all over the place and making the Ark so merry I could hardly stand it."

"When can I take him home?" Miss Barnworth asked breathlessly. "I'll have to find a basket and—"

"Right now you can take him," Mrs. Noah interrupted hastily. "You go out and talk to the Captain and I'll have my sons, Shem, Ham, and Japheth, put on their gloves and put him in a box." She smiled at Angela. "They always wear their gloves when they handle this delicate, smiling creature because they don't want to bruise him."

Old Cat, growling and fighting, was crammed into the box and the lid secured with a piece of stout rope. Shem, redfaced and perspiring profusely but cowed by his mother's threatening tongue, went with Miss Barnworth to carry the box to Canaan Common.

Tripping gaily along by his side, she bombarded Shem with hundreds of questions about Old Cat's diet, grooming and care—which Shem answered in grunts and monosyllables. His full attention was given to a hole in the box. Through this, Old Cat had thrust a paw—and, with nails extended, was probing for Shem's leg.

He scored a bullseye as they were crossing Eighth Millennium Circle and Shem gave a scream of anguish. It was unheard, however, by either Miss Barnworth or passersby. The Choir of the Apostles had a rehearsal room on that block—and the featured soprano, who had a range of six octaves, had just hit her highest note. Shem's yelp blended perfectly.

In her beautiful house, Miss Barnworth removed the lid

from the box—and Old cat leaped out and disappeared like a streak of ink under a chest of drawers.

She sat down on the floor and she coaxed and pleaded—but Old Cat refused to show even a whisker. She whispered baby talk; she rolled paper into a ball and moved it enticingly along the edge of the chest; she warmed milk and put it in a fragile porcelain bowl on a silver tray. Old Cat remained silent and unmoved in his dark retreat.

Angela Barnworth spent the whole eternal day trying to make friends with Old Cat. Then, discouraged and dispirited, she went to bed. It took her a long time to go to sleep—because she believed there was something in her makeup that made her repugnant to cats. Tomorrow—well, perhaps tomorrow, she could think of something to make herself more appealing...

Old Cat waited until he thought it was safe and then made a complete tour of the house. Everything was closed up tight—there was no escape. He came back to the porcelain bowl and drank the milk—glaring all the while at Miss Barnworth's sleeping form. Then, disdaining to wash the milk spatters from his face, he crawled back into his hiding place.

The next morning, Miss Barnworth went down to the Ararat Pet Shop, which is directly across from the Ark and run by Captain Noah's grandson, Javan. Here, she spent a great many blessings on a ball, a scratch post, and a delightful feeding bowl—which, filled with milk and then lapped to the bottom, revealed the message— "Good Morning, Dear Friend!"

Old Cat was unimpressed. Even though Miss Barnworth rolled and bounced the ball—even though she ruined her nails demonstrating the scratch post—even though she drank a full quart of milk to show how the heartwarming greeting appeared almost like magic—Old Cat stayed under the chest.

On that celestial night, it took even longer for Miss Barnworth to go to sleep. *It's my fault*, she thought. *It's my fault he doesn't love me. All my life I've wanted to be loved—but nobody really has. I've bought presents for people but the things you buy don't count. It's the little things that aren't worth a penny—the thoughtful things that people don't expect, that make you necessary and wanted. Maybe a nod when they're feeling lonely—or a nothing-at-all silence that lets them know you understand—or a warmth you can feel going out through your skin and into their hearts.* Miss Barnworth tossed and turned—but in the night, an idea came to her for a truly extravagant but doesn't-cost-a-penny present for Old Cat.

The following day, Miss Barnworth sang as she dressed. She put on her most comfortable shoes and her gardening frock, hat, and gloves.

She warmed some milk and put it in Old Cat's bowl by the side of the chest. "You just wait!" she called softly. "I'm going to bring you a surprise!"

Then, all aglow with enthusiasm, she went out of her beautiful house. Hurrying across the Celestial City, she came at last to the Elysian Fields—where she started her search for a nice bed of catnip.

Old Cat waited until Miss Barnworth's heels had tick-ticked beyond range of his extremely sensitive auditory apparatus before emerging from his stronghold.

He had decided that there was only one sure way to win his freedom. He would mutilate, tear, mangle, rip, and ruin!

He would make a mess of this orderly prison—and his jailer would be so angry and outraged that she'd be glad to get rid of him!

With one swipe of his paw, Old Cat overturned the bowl and the milk went rippling across the rug. He attacked his scratch post and clawed it to shreds. He jumped up on the mantel and sent the clock and the ornaments flying—saving the fragile porcelain bowl on its silver tray till the last and yowled fiendishly as it crashed and splintered.

He assaulted the drapes on the windows and tore them into long streamers. With tooth and nail, he ripped pillows to shreds and the feathers flew through the house like a snow-storm. He pulled pictures from the walls, knocked bottles from their shelves and loved every minute of his work.

When Miss Barnworth returned, he was resting in his hiding place under the chest. He heard her utter a cry of horror as she saw the chaos that he had created. Then she dropped something on the floor, threw herself on the bed and started to cry as though she'd never stop.

This was a great disappointment to Old Cat. He had expected an open window and a broom-swat which would catapult him to liberty. Suddenly, a delicious smell was wafted to his disgruntled nose. It had an insidious come-hither aroma that pulled him out of his lair inch by inch. It came from the paper bag that Miss Barnworth had dropped on the floor. Old Cat crouched over it and inhaled deeply. Catnip. Exquisite, delectable, ambrosial catnip.

Catnip, in former times, had always sent Old Cat into a maudlin state of delirium. Happy fancies had raced through his muddled head—wonderful adventures in which he was

Lord High Cat of the alleys.

But this catnip was different. Instead of being lifted into a beautiful dream, Old Cat was crushed beneath a nightmare. He felt the pain of every foot that had kicked him—every stone that had struck him—every stick that had hit him. He shivered and shook as he relived every night of cold and sleet and rain. All the old wounds on his scarred body seemed to become new again—and the pain was so intense that Old Cat opened his mouth and screamed at the form on the bed to help him.

But Miss Barnworth didn't understand. She rose from the bed and threw open the window.

"All right!" she cried. "If you hate me so much and you want to go—then go! I want you to go—do you hear— because I hate you, too!"

She dropped on the bed, buried her face in the pillow and went on weeping. To Old Cat she sounded like a small, distressed kitten. He rose and walked on noiseless feet around the room. It took several minutes to find the ball. He picked it up in his mouth and jumped up on the bed.

He approached warily. He laid the ball on the pillow and watched it roll down and hit her shoulder. She didn't move— but she did stop crying.

Well... he was too tired to play ball, anyway. Old Cat turned around three times and curled up with his back against Miss Barnworth's stomach. He heard her sigh—and in a moment, he felt her hand stroking his side. It felt real good.

Tomorrow, he'd take a bath. A full bath—behind the ears, between the toes, and to tip of tail. If you belonged, a cat had to take some pride in himself.

Angela Barnworth and Old Cat.

Old Cat wiggled his back into a closer fit with Miss Barnworth's stomach and started to purr.

He hadn't used his song of contentment for many a year—and it sounded like an ungreased porch swing.

However, to Angela Barnworth, it was the most wonderful music ever heard in paradise.

What more could anyone want in this Celestial City.

She had a house.

And a cat.

And love.

III

The efficient and punctual Department of Celestial Transport had never been in such a mess. At times of disaster on earth—such as the eruption of Mount Vesuvius or the Great Plague in London, when the renowned transit system had been taxed to its very limit to carry the thousands of immigrants to the Celestial City, it had functioned superbly. The carriers, dripping water like gigantic silver whales from their passage through the barrier of morning mist at the rim of the universe, had arrived and departed on a split-second schedule.

At the present moment, cruising in aimless circles in that wet, opaque cloud, there were eight over due carriers impatiently awaiting clearance to descend and disembark passengers at the Stairs.

Otto Schnitter's school bus was the yellow thumb in the machinery. As jolly and unconcerned as a Halloween pumpkin, it occupied the landing area—its semaphores crying "STOP" to every eye and every light red flashing as though it had an acute case of tic douloureux.

"Where is Mr. Schnitter?" demanded the frenzied Phut, Schedular Chief in Charge. "Hasn't anyone even seen him?"

"I saw him," said Senior Saint Peter. "He came up the Stairs with his usual crowd of children about half an hour or so ago. He went through the Gates with them and hasn't come back."

"This is an absolutely horrendous situation!" cried Phut. "What are we going to do to get those carriers in?"

"Please, sir—," a little man with watery, benevolent eyes pushed his way through the crowd, "if I might make a suggestion. What you need, it seems to me, is another flight of Stairs! One for the school bus and one for the carriers! My name is Sek and my friends and I love to get together on such projects and—"

"Mr. Sek—," shouted Phut, "we do not need another flight of Stairs! And if you and your Shinar mates show up here with even one piece of lumber, I'll confiscate it! There's nothing we need less than a Stair of Babel! Now please— everybody—go and look for Otto Schnitter—and for the love of my schedule—find him!"

When they started the search, Mr. Schnitter and Sukie were at the Ark of Captain and Mrs. Noah on the Street of Miracles. In a county court house in far away New Hampshire, her name was Susan Kathryn Fordan, and she had just celebrated her sixth birthday this past tenth day of October. Her name was almost longer than she was tall—and so her parents, who were heartbroken at this moment because they were quite unaware that she was in the capable hands of Otto Schnitter—had shortened it to "Sukie."

To the swaggering Don Juans of the first grade, she had been a femme fatale; red hair that made an astrakhan cap for her head, brown eyes that became inverted half-moons when she laughed and quarter-moons when she wept—and a mouth that was most charming even when it was messed up from eating a chocolate ice cream bar. Her snub nose had an abundance of freckles—as though she had run headlong into a handful of brown confetti.

Mr. Schnitter had had no intention of visiting Captain Noah's Ark. By this time, Sukie should have been in the care of one of the grandmothers of Angels' Aide, where temporary orphans of the Celestial City are lovingly housed until claimed by a close relative. And his school bus, instead of discombobulating traffic at the foot of the Stairs, should have been in its special "No Trespassing" parking place in the shadow of the mighty wall of Heaven.

This time consuming detour by the way of Captain Noah's animal shelter had been caused by a question that old Ott had put to Sukie on the journey from earth.

The school bus had been rollicking along on this fine October morning—just as it did every day in the year—the children laughing and playing and singing. Arriving at the brand new and stately viaduct, arching high and far on a spiral nebula, Mr. Schnitter had driven to the top and stopped. He was exceedingly proud of this viaduct because he had insisted that it be built as a safety measure for his school bus. Cobbled with small stars, it arched over the main and busy path of the not-a-second-to-lose Intercosmic and Intergalactic Comet System, Unlimited.

"Look!" Mr. Schnitter had called to the children, pointing his finger. "Here comes one!"

A great ball of fire, switching its flaming tail, had come roaring down the path, passed under the viaduct and disappeared.

"What was that?" Sukie had asked.

"That was a comet," old Ott had replied.

"It looked like Herbie—only a lot, lot bigger."

"Who—," and this had been the question that old Ott should not have asked, "Who is Herbie?"

"He was my guppy."

"Oh." Mr. Schnitter had nodded his head. "Herbie the guppy—and he was comet-shape?"

"Sort of." Sukie's eyes had grown sad. "He died. Me and my best friend Doris—we had a funeral for him out in the back yard. She wanted to put him in a box—but I wouldn't let her. I put him in a Mason jar filled up with spring water—like he always liked to swim in. And I put a tag on the jar with his name—Herbie. Why did he die? Didn't he know how much I liked him?"

"Why, Herbie's not defunct!" Mr. Schnitter had comforted. "I saw him just yesterday—swimming around his jar like he was on a merry-go-round! He's at the Ark on the Street of Miracles with all the other pets—just wiggling his fins and waiting for you to claim him!"

"You're not fooling?" Sukie had asked.

"You just wait and see if I'm fooling!" old Ott had laughed. "As soon as you get settled, I'll take you to the Ark myself!"

"What about Picklepuss?"

"Picklepuss?" Mr. Schnitter had elevated his eyebrows, which Mrs. Noah said reminded her of two white caterpillars in the molting season. "What in thunder is a picklepuss?"

"He's a turtle. Real extra little. My Uncle Carl—who is real extra fat—rocked on him with a chair and Picklepuss got cracked and died, too."

"I see."

"Will Picklepuss be at that place where Herbie is?"

"Did you like him?"

"Yes."

"Take my word for it—" Ott had spun the wheel for the final turn and headed down the long straight skyway toward the Celestial City. "That turtle Picklepuss has been waiting and wondering where you are—and his heart's going to jump right out through his shell for joy when he sees you!"

"I'm glad." Sukie had curled up in the seat next to him. "Real glad." She had tried to cover a large yawn with a too small hand. "Excuse me." Her eyes had closed slowly. "I told my best friend—when I grow up to be a mother—instead of children, I'm going to have turtles—just like Picklepuss—lots and scads of little green turtles..."

When Mr. Schnitter had shepherded his brood of small fry up the Stairs to the great Gates, he had discovered that Sukie possessed a determination that was as towering and as immovable as an alp. In spite of all the gentle coaxing of Mrs. Elvira Hunt, her assigned grandmother, she had clung to old Ott like a fierce little bramble bush—soaking his broad shoulder with tears and refusing to go anywhere until she had seen and collected Herbie and Picklepuss.

So Ott, with Grandmother Hunt trotting at his heels, had carried Sukie across the Plaza of Eternity and down the Street of Miracles to Number 10. Now, he stood regarding his heavy gold watch with a weighty frown—while Sukie gazed tenderly and lovingly upon her two friends in their private little heavens, the guppy in his jar and the turtle on his rock in a water-filled bowl.

"I just have to move that school bus!" said Mr. Schnitter.

"You run right along," replied Grandmother Hunt. "I'm sure I can manage things from now on."

"But you've only got two arms," argued Ott. "You can't carry Sukie and a guppy and a turtle!"

"I'll get Davy to help out," said Captain Noah. "He's been hanging around here all afternoon. Oh, Davy!" he called to the other room, "Will you come here a minute?" He turned to Ott and wagged his head. "Davy's got a terrible problem living in a house full of women. If it isn't Abigail it's Ahinoam—and if it isn't Ahinoam it's Michal telling him how he ought to behave and conduct himself like a retired king. Oh, there you are, Davy!" he cried to a ruddy-faced individual who had appeared in the doorway. "Would you mind carrying this bowl and jar for Grandmother Hunt out to the Avenue of Compassion and Third Millennium Circle?"

"Be glad to," answered Davy in the clipped manner of a soldier—and with Grandmother Hunt trying to keep up with his long strides, off they went down the Street of Miracles and onto Eden Way.

"Be careful and don't slop the water!" admonished Sukie. "Were you really a king, Mr. Davy?"

"I was," said Davy.

"You don't look like one."

"Well, I'm not dressed for it. That's what the women are always after me about. Wear this—don't wear that—stand up straight—don't slouch—don't scratch your head. They seem to think that no part of a king ever itches. But it does. It itches like sixty."

"Didn't you like being a king?"

"No—can't say that I did. I liked being a soldier. Now and then, I go out to Peaceful Reveille to drive the smell of women's perfume out of my nose and sniff the good honest odor of fighting men. Not that we have too much in common! They can spin tales for hours about the siege of Antioch—or the battle of Tannenberg—or Gettysburg—or Verdun—or Iwo Jima. But they're a bunch of youngsters! Hardly a one of 'em has ever heard about my great victory over the Philistines on the plain at Keilah!"

"How did you start being a soldier?" asked Sukie. "Did you go to school?"

"School? Of course not!" Davy snorted his disdain. "It just came naturally! I was just a shepherd boy—big and strong for my age, of course, when I did my first fighting. No sword—no spear—no armor! Not a blessed thing to protect myself but my shepherd's bag of brook stones and my—"

"Here we are at last!" interrupted Grandmother Hunt, opening the gate of Angels' Aide. "Say 'thank you' to the nice gentleman, Sukie."

"Thank you, Mr. Davy," said Sukie. "And sometime I'd

89

like you to tell me some soldier stories."

"Any time. Any time at all." He gave them a stiff salute. "Good evening, ladies!" Turning on his heel, he went off at a martial pace down Third Millennium Circle.

Sukie, as the days passed, grew very fond of the cherub shelter and its legion of cheerful, indulgent grandmothers. Her room could have been the one she had slept in in far-off New Hampshire. Mother Goose characters romped gaily on the wallpaper. The rag rug had the same hooped-up place that her father was forever stumbling over when he had come to end her day with a favorite read-me-to-sleep story. The bed, dresser, and table were the identical luscious shade of strawberry ice cream soda pink with the white rose decals— one decal a trifle crooked because her mother had sneezed just as it had been applied—and Sukie and her father had hooted and laughed and said that the roses were so real looking she must have come down with a rose allergy.

Even better than bedtime stories were her secret visits with Otto Schnitter, whose window faced hers across the wide Avenue of Compassion. She had elected him her favorite person. Every afternoon, she made it a point to be standing outside Luke's dispensary where the stairs led up to Otto's apartment, to engage him in serious conversation. They spoke of the weather—which was always perfect. Of each other's health—which was constantly perfect. And of the state of the Celestial City—which was perpetually perfect.

But the most exciting visits were the clandestine ones that came in the evening after Grandmother Hunt had tucked her into bed. The moment the door closed behind her, Sukie was out from under the covers and flying across the room to the window. Then, chin resting on hands, she stared down the avenue—waiting for the distant and thimble-sized figures of Mr. Schnitter and his dog, Spot, to appear in the silver circle of light of the furthest street lamp.

It was their habit, after a shared dinner, to stroll down to the Gates. Here, Mr. Schnitter checked his school bus from head-lamp to tail lamp to be sure it was clean, safe and fueled for tomorrow's trip—while Spot raced up and down Francis' huge carrier, standing ready to depart, his sniffs taking hundreds of nose pictures of last night's passengers.

After that, they always walked through the great Plaza of Eternity, nodding a head and wagging a tail at friends and acquaintances. Now and then, they might stop to pass a few words with Captain Cyrus Skinner, in from Fiddlers' Green with his ship's cat on his shoulder—or with Joseph, a quiet, humble man, who made beautiful things out of wood in his carpenter shop on the Avenue of Adoration.

Leaving the Plaza, they crossed Eden Way—Mr. Schnitter keeping Spot in check because it was always busy and crowded at this early evening hour. Then, before starting down the Avenue of Justice, old Ott invariably stopped and spent a blessing on two milk-and-honeys on a stick—one for himself and one for Spot.

These eaten and fingers and paws licked, they ambled down the Avenue of Justice to the large and sprawling building which stands behind the Bureau of Recording Angels on First Millennium Circle.

This houses the famous Department of Petitions and Tokens of Remembrance and it is fully staffed throughout every hour of the celestial day and night.

At the very beginning of all things, it had been recognized that there must be some means of communication between the Celestial City and the most unbelievable distant whirling sphere. Sound had been created—but sound was such a plodder it would require aeons piled up on top of aeons to cross unlimited space. Light, too, had been born—but its hundred and eighty-six thousand miles a second was a paltry snail's pace to conquer infinity.

It was then, to solve this dilemma, that the Proprietor created thought and gave it to every individual wherever he or she might be—for thought is instantaneous. It ignores and laughs at every rule of speed and distance. It can travel as far and as wide as the thinker wishes in less than a wink of the thinker's eye.

To receive, classify and allocate these thoughts—which in a single celestial day sweep in like flakes in a driving snow-storm—this Department of Petitions and Tokens of Remembrance was established. Most petitions, asking a particular favor from the Proprietor, come in during the dark hours of a sphere—because people are inclined to whisper a wish or desire before going to sleep. Tokens of Remembrance come in at all hours because the thought of an absent one can spring from a broken toy in an attic—or a cane in a closet—or a diary that ends in the middle of a sentence.

The Department was one of Mr. Schnitter's favorite places. He loved to cast an eye over the day's business and see if he could discover any familiar name. Since Sukie's arrival, he always looked for anything that might interest her, too. Tonight was a good night.

"Look at this, Spot!" he chuckled. "Mrs. Robinson petitioning for help on her mixed pickle entry for the county fair! And remember that skinny Perkins boy? No— 'course you don't—he's long after your time—but anyway, he's skinny as a snake and he's asking for his pimples to go away before the freshman dance come Friday. Must have a new girl. Oh—look here—something for Sukie! Now that's real nice, wouldn't you say? Yes, sir—and here's another one! Come on, now—you and me'd better get along out there and tell her so's she'll have something nice to dream on."

Mr. Schnitter and his dog had some trouble making their way along First Millennium Circle because of the many people arriving for the evening performance of the Theater of Genesius. Turning into the Avenue of Compassion and with Spot setting the pace, it took only a few minutes to reach Angels' Aide and Sukie's window.

"Hi, there!" old Ott called softly.

"Hi, Mr. Schnitter! Did I get any tokens today?"

"You sure did! Two of 'em!"

"Who from?"

"Well—you remember Ben Fitz—the custodian at your school? He dressed up a little today 'cause there was a Parent-Teacher meeting. He wore that tie you gave him last Christmas—and while he was tying it, he said to his wife— 'Y'know—I really miss seeing that little Sukie around the school—she was a real whizzer.'"

"He called me that?" said Sukie in an awed voice. "Why, Mr. Fitz never called anybody or anything that except his new floor polisher!"

"Well, you're right up there, neck and neck with the

93

polisher in Mr. Fitz' esteem! I'm right proud, myself, to know a genuine whizzer. And here's another token that I call A-Number One! Remember that old white horse?"

"That belonged to the junk man? That I used to feed sugar?"

"The same. He stopped in front of your house this morning and refused to budge an inch. Pasted right on his horse mind and framed by his long ears, was a thought picture of you holding out your hand."

"I think—" Sukie sighed, "I think that's just lovely."

"I couldn't agree with you more," said Mr. Schnitter. "Now you go to bed."

"Good night, Mr. Schnitter—and thank you."

"Good night," he called. "And pleasant dreams."

Old Ott's parting wish was fully granted. She dreamed of Grandmother Hunt, Mr. Davy, a white horse, Otto Schnitter, Captain Noah, Spot and Mr. Fitz. It was one of the best dreams she had ever dreamt because every one of them loved her.

The days passed swiftly and soon it was near to Christmas—a holiday that is kept joyously, reverently, and completely in the Celestial City. It was here, within these mighty timeless walls, that Christmas had its beginning. This is the font—the source—the wellspring of all the Christmases, past and present, of that small planet Earth, so greatly favored by the Proprietor.

Star candles were placed in the windows of every building and dwelling from the great Wall to the far limits of this incredible, breathtaking metropolis—silver wreaths with golden hollyberries hung on every door—millions on millions of yards of rainbows were strung across the wide avenues from street lamp to street lamp—and the massive Gates to the Celestial City were almost obscured by the vast number of cherub stockings, of every size and color, that had been hung there to be filled with blessings on Christmas Eve.

Once again, the Angels of the Holy Night were at work far out beyond the Elysian Fields—making ready the great Star of Bethlehem. On this Eve of Christmas—as it had almost two thousand other Eves—it would rise in all its glory, its brilliance still undimmed by passing years, to stand and bathe every roof and spire and tower of the Celestial City with its clear and beckoning light.

Angels' Aide, too, made its preparations for Christmas and it became a cherub-hive of activity. Every dear friend must be remembered. Sukie made out her list:

> *Grandmother Hunt—hankacheef for waving not blowing.*
> *Mr. Davy—embroydered sheep bag with some nice stones.*
> *Mr. Schnitter—slippers, yellow-bus color, real big.*
> *Captain Noah—one box of ship biscutts.*
> *Spot—chocklit flaver bean bag for ketching.*

One celestial day, when on earth it was mid-December, Grandmother Hunt gave Sukie a small pail.

"Come, dear," she said, "we're all going out to get stardust!"

"Why are we going to do that?" asked Sukie.

"It's an old custom that's been going on I don't know how many years," explained Grandmother Hunt. "Right this minute, the Angels of the Holy Night are dusting and polishing the Bethlehem Star so's no other star will be as bright on Christmas Eve. They save every speck of dust and give it to you cherubs."

"What do we do with it?"

"You bring it back here. Then you mix it with water, shape it into a little star and bake it in the sun."

"Then do I put it in my room?"

"Oh, my no!" laughed Grandmother Hunt. "It's a present. For your father and mother. It'll be sent down just before Christmas with all the other little stars, by very special delivery. Your star will be hung right over your house in New Hampshire."

"Will anybody know it's there?"

"Well, I just guess they will! Didn't you ever notice, when you went out walking at Christmastime, that there was just one house—in whole blocks and blocks of houses—that looked more Christmasy than any of the others? The holly wreaths had the greenest leaves and the reddest berries! Every window candle had a merry, joy-to-the-world flame! Not one branch of the evergreen had slooped under the weight of all its ornaments—and the tree stood there as proud as one of the three kings to be a part of Christmas!"

"Yes, I have," said Sukie.

"If you'd looked up, you'd have seen a cherub's star right over the rooftop."

"I'm going to make the best one that was ever made!" boasted Sukie. "When I was littler, I used to make real good mud pies. And pies are harder than stars because they're not supposed to have points."

It was a beautiful day for stardust gathering. The grandmothers had borrowed three great harvest wagons from Peaceful Pastures and had them floored with fresh cut hay. To pull them, Shard, Crag, and Shale, the Proprietor's chariot drivers, had brought the mighty horses from the Stables on Eden Way. Each gigantic steed seemed to know that the journey must be happy and safe for not one monstrous nostril breathed fire and each fearsome hoof, which could strike lightning, was put down as softly as a kitten's.

Sukie came back with her pail, her hair, and her eyebrows filled with stardust. When she leaned out the window for her nightly chat with Mr. Schnitter, she looked like a tinseled Christmas tree ornament. She had a hard time getting to sleep—her mind insisting on planning each angle and each point for the finest star that ever hung over anybody's house anytime anywhere.

Early the next morning, she set to work. First, she sifted the stardust through the seat of her Sunday-best underpants to be sure there wasn't a lump. Then, drop by drop and stirring continuously, she added water. In time, it reached a sticky state halfway between liquification and solidification— just the right consistency, she had learned from past experience, to construct an outstanding mud pie.

The delicate job of starmaking now began. Red hair on end and brows furrowed, Sukie kneaded, pinched, poked, pressed, thumped, prodded, patted, punched, squeezed, pounded, flattened, smoothed, buffed, and polished. All this required a full celestial day—but at long and exhausted last, the lump of star-clay had become a reasonable facsimile of the great Star of Bethlehem.

Carefully, because her creation was in a very flabby and spongy state, she transferred it to a sunny spot on her window sill. Here, Grandmother Hunt had assured her—between

*Sukie works diligently on her Christmas star as
Grandmother Hunt looks on.*

Herbie the guppy's Mason jar and Picklepuss the turtle's bowl—it would bake hard and bright. In three days, on the Eve of Christmas, she could carry it down to the Gates—and the Star Hangers would put it aboard the swift, evergreen-decorated carrier. On Christmas Day, it would shine over her parent's house and passersby would envy the people who lived there.

That night, at Angels' Aide, when all the cherubs and grandmothers were sound asleep, there was one who remained wide awake. It was most annoying because he had never been troubled with insomnia. In fact, unless he happened to be lying on a sharp pebble, he had been able to drop off with no trouble at all at any hour of the day or night.

But he wasn't lying on a pebble. He was stretched out on his nice, downy, smooth rock that was surrounded by his own moat of tepid water—which couldn't drain away because it was dyked by the rim of his bowl.

With all this and heaven, too—Picklepuss was unable to drift off to dreamland. He tried counting water striders skipping over the surface of a pond—but that didn't work. It made him more alert. He lifted his head and inhaled.

Ah! That was it! It was a smell that was keeping him awake! A smell that every turtle recognizes the moment he hatches. Mud. Fresh, wonderful, delightful, satisfying mud! Picklepuss slid from his rock, swam his moat and assaulted the rampart of his bowl.

It required a superturtle effort to overcome this obstacle—but with turtle tenacity, he rolled over the rim like a minute armored tank. Then, coming upon Sukie's star, waiting to be baked by tomorrow's sun, Picklepuss oozed, burrowed and pressed until he was buried in delicious mud. All that was exposed to the night air was one sixteenth of an inch of turtle tail.

Next morning, Sukie discovered the abandoned rock and the empty bowl. Her heartbroken cries and wails broke the terrible news to Angels' Aide and most of the Avenue of Compassion. Her room and the bushes under her window were carefully searched—and then the cherub shelter was turned upside down and inside out in the frantic search for Picklepuss.

Mr. Schnitter and Mr. Davy crawled over the whole playground on their hands and knees. Dysmas, the thief, examined the roof and climbed down and up every one of the many chimneys. Sek and his Shinar friends sifted every scrap basket and rubbish pail. Old Cat climbed every nearby tree and searched every limb. Gideon Jones came with his trumpet and softly played a levee tune to charm Picklepuss from his hiding place. Angels' Aide looked as though it were under a state of siege because the Angels of Peace had roped off the avenue from Second to Fourth Millennium Circle to prevent any heedless foot from flattening the missing Picklepuss.

Unaware of all this furious activity, the lost turtle slept blissfully within Sukie's Christmas Star—wiggling a foot, now and then, as the material baked and became less comfortable. Instinct kept knocking on his snit of a brain to tell him that this was not a good place to hibernate—but Picklepuss was too lethargic to listen.

On the morning of the third day, the search was reluctantly abandoned. Grandmother Hunt put a black mourning ribbon around Picklepuss' empty bowl and tied it in a drooping, tearful bow. A service was conducted by Mr. Davy—who expressed the hope that the little turtle had gone on to a better world. No one knew of one beyond heaven—but it was possible that the Proprietor, who worked in strange ways to perform his wonders, might have created one for good citizens of the halfshell such as Picklepuss.

That late afternoon, on the Eve of Christmas, a much subdued and red-eyed Sukie, accompanied by Otto Schnitter and Mr. Davy, set out for the Gates with her Christmas Star. Never before had she seen such a multitude of people so merry or so laden down with bundles and parcels and packages in the brightest of holiday wrappings. Even with Mr. Schnitter's broad shoulders to clear the way, they needed an hour to reach the great Plaza of Eternity.

It was then that Mr. Davy decided that they could make better time if he carried Sukie—so he hoisted her up on his shoulders and they pushed on across the Plaza—Sukie holding her star over her head so that it wouldn't be crushed or crumbled.

"Look!" someone would shout in the tight-packed throng. "It's just like on that first Christmas Eve! That little star's going to Bethlehem!"

"It's going to my mother and father!" called Sukie. "That is it's going if we can just get to the Gates!"

"We'll get there, all right!" said Ott. "Make way—make way!" he called.

"Mr. Schnitter! Oh, Mr. Schnitter!" cried a distraught voice.

"What?" shouted Ott. "Who said that?"

"I did!" Miss Barnworth, Old Cat's mistress, pushed her way between two burly cometmongers like a limp dishrag emerging from between the rollers of a washing machine ringer. She righted her hat and blew the hair out of her eyes. "Mr. Schnitter—I know the whereabouts of Picklepuss! I've just come back from the Down of Promise!"

"What's out there?" asked Mr. Davy.

"That's where Solomon lives! Solomon, the Wise! It came to me that if he could decide the mother of a child—he surely ought to be able to find a turtle!"

"So what did Solomon say?"

"Well—" Miss Barnworth paused to gulp a breath, "after I gave him all the facts, he went into deep thought! And I do mean deep! It was just as though he'd dived headfirst into a lake and was never coming up! Then—he opened his eyes—and do you know what he said?" She lifted an arm and pointed dramatically. "He said Picklepuss was in the middle of Sukie's Christmas Star!"

"My star?" Sukie held it up so she could examine it.

"Nonsense!" scoffed Mr. Davy.

"Fiddlesticks!" snorted Otto Schnitter.

"No it's not fiddle nonsticks!" cried Sukie. "He is in my star! Look—" she pointed to the one sixteenth of an inch of tail that Picklepuss had neglected to tuck in. "This is the end of Picklepuss' train that he's so proud of!"

"Oh, my Christmas lights and carols!" groaned Mr. Schnitter.

"How are we going to get him out?" laughed Sukie.

"I was afraid you were going to ask that," said old Ott. "Well—there's a fellow I know on the Avenue of Adoration who might be able to do it. 'Course he might not even be there—being so late and Christmas Eve besides. But we can see—come on, follow me!"

So off they went—back across the Plaza; old Ott carrying Sukie and Miss Barnworth hanging onto Mr. Davy's coattail. Another full hour passed before they entered the carpenter shop on the Avenue of Adoration.

"Do you think you can get my turtle out?" asked Sukie. "Without hurting the star, I mean? That's very important because it's got to be sent off tonight so it can hang over my mother's house!"

"Oh, I'm sure it can be done," said Joseph, in his gentle way. He picked up a miniature saw and set to work. "This is a very fine star, if you don't mind me saying so."

"Is it like the Bethlehem Star?"

"Exactly. And I ought to know. I saw that old star when it was very new." The small star became two half-stars. Joseph picked up Picklepuss and put him in Sukie's hand. "There we are. Now, a little glue—" With deft hands, he applied a brush and then fitted the two halves together. "And it's good as new, I should say. Now—you'd better hurry on down to the Gates! It's almost time for the carrier to leave!"

"Thank you, Mr. Joseph!" called Sukie, as she, Ott, Davy and Miss Barnworth hurried out the door. "I'll remember you always—and Picklepuss, too!"

Joseph watched them disappear into the crowd. Then he closed the door of his carpenter shop and walked swiftly toward the Street of Miracles with a smile on his face. It was Christmas Eve and his wife, Mary, was waiting for him.

To Otto Schnitter's dismay, the Plaza was even more tightly filled with Christmas-makers than it had been on their first visit. He pushed and bellowed and shoved and shouted.

Miss Barnworth was lost before they reached Eden Lane. Squeezed between a tree and a brawny halosmith, she was left with Davy's coattail in her hands.

"Women!" panted Davy, as they ran through the Gates and down the broad Stairs. "Wouldn't you think she'd have sense enough to let loose my coattail before she ripped it off?" He stopped and stared with disbelief. "Why—where's the carrier?"

"It's gone!" cried Ott. "We're too late!" He pointed. "Just a couple of minutes too late! There it is up there!"

The enormous carrier, bathed in the light of the great Star of Bethlehem which was rising over the Elysian Fields to shine on the Celestial City, hung above the stars like a gleaming Christmas tree ornament. It hovered motionless, awaiting a signal from Phut, Schedular Chief in Charge, that the way was clear through the bank of mist on the rim of the universe. One doorway still stood open and black against the amber glow within, the figure of a Star Hanger raised his arm and waved to the three on the Stairs.

"Come back! Come back!" shouted Sukie. "You can't leave without my star!"

"He can't hear you," old Ott said mournfully. "And even if he could, he couldn't come back. It'd upset the whole schedule."

"But my star!" wept Sukie. "I worked so hard to make it just right! If it doesn't hang over my mother's house it'll be just a regular Christmas and not something special!"

"Here—hand it over to me!" said Mr. Davy.

"What are you going to do?" asked old Ott. "There's just no way I can see to—"

"I'm going to shoot it right in that doorway, that's what I'm going to do!" snapped Mr. Davy. He took a long thong from his coat pocket and fitted it to Sukie's star. "Now, stand back!"

"But if you miss!" worried Otto Schnitter. "If you—"

"I don't ever miss!" growled Davy. "Didn't you ever hear how, when I was a mere sprout, with this here sling I knocked the daylights out of Goliath?"

He began whirling the sling around his head—faster and faster until Sukie's star made a continuous ribbon of light like a giant halo. The thong, cutting the air, hummed—then sang—then screamed—then shrieked in such a shrill and piercing voice that Sukie covered her ears.

He was not Mr. Davy now—he was David, the shepherd boy, every young muscle knotted with strain, on a long-gone day in the valley of Elah.

Then he released the star from the sling—and it sped like a small meteor through the darkness. Upward and outward and as truly aimed as the brook stone had been from his shepherd's bag in that olden time. It flew through the door of the hovering carrier and was caught by the Star Hanger.

And not a moment too soon. Phut had just given the all-clear signal. With a final wave of his hand, the Star Hanger closed the door—and the great Christmas carrier, at tremendous speed, vanished from sight into the thick bank of mist on the rim of the universe...

It was a wonderful Christmas down at Sukie's house in New Hampshire. Never before had the holly wreathes had such green leaves or such fat, red berries. Never, in anyone's memory, had the window candles had such a joy-to-the-world

Sukie's star shines bright above her parents' house
on Christmas Eve.

flame. And the tree, laden with its lights and ornaments, stood as proud as one of the three kings to be a part of Christmas. People came for miles just to look at Sukie's house—and to envy her father and mother, who lived there.

These two, of course, missed Sukie very much. On that calm, silent night, they went out onto the porch and they stood there with their arms around one another.

They looked up toward the Celestial City—as people often do when they are troubled—and they saw a bright little star shining merrily and lovingly over their roof.

It's quite possible that they knew who sent it.

They were most familiar with Sukie's mud pies—and a child's mud pie and a cherub's star are much alike.

For, after all, a cherub's star is a mere mud pie with points.

IV

Countless stories have been written and told about the Flying Dutchman. Sailors, who are a superstitious lot, will swear that it is a ghost-ship—and its appearance is a dire omen of impending disaster.

This dreadful specter of the high seas is commanded by Captain Vanderdecken—who, for some vile and unmentionable misdemeanor, has been condemned to sail on and on forever, without the slightest hope of ever making port.

Anyone in the Celestial City knows that these earthside yarns are as false as a square halo. Captain Vanderdecken is a happy-go-lucky and respected citizen of Fiddlers' Green, which lies just beyond the last millennium circle of the Avenue of Compassion.

This great, heavenlocked harbor draws a large number of

visitors on a fine Sunday afternoon. Tied up or drifting at anchor are galleons, brigantines, sloops, schooners, liners, rowboats, barges, skiffs, windjammers, tugs, trawlers, sampans, junks, freighters, scows, tankers and every sort and size of ship of war. Each one seems to bow or curtsy to the visitors—as if it was eager to say, "Look at me! Please look at me! Am I not as beautiful as I was on that day I married the ocean, sea, river, lake or pond? Just see—I've brought those who trusted me to safe harbor!"

Many visitors, because of the wild and fanciful stories they have heard or read, wish to see the Flying Dutchman. Between voyages, she is to be found at her wharf in Big Fisherman Bight—and Captain Vanderdecken, a genial hogshead of a man, is delighted to show off the Dutch apple cake order of his vessel.

Laughter rumbles deep in the hogshead—and then roars out through his black-thicket beard like a foghorn. They say it can easily be heard over the deafening pandemonium of the most vicious storm—and many of these ships, finding themselves tortured beyond endurance by typhoon or hurricane, followed that foghorn bellow and the Flying Dutchman to drop anchor in the tranquil waters of Fiddlers' Green.

There is another falsehood in the earthside yarns about the Flying Dutchman. They say it plies the oceans and the seven seas—but never ventures on any inland waters. This is simply not true. It is written, in Captain Vanderdecken's log, that on a memorable night—a spring night on the Proprietor's well-loved planet Earth—the Flying Dutchman sailed up a major river of its western hemisphere. Under an Easter moon, the good Captain sweated mightily as he guided his beloved ship up the muddy stream on this unprecedented voyage. Never again, he vowed, never again would he do anything so foolish—not even for Easter and Gideon Jones.

Gid was a comparative newcomer to the Celestial City. He came from New Orleans and he believed that there was no finer place anywhere.

Anybody, according to Gid, could find anything he wanted for his body and soul in New Orleans. It was old lace and hot jazz. It was neon glare and warm candlelight. It was the frantic present and the faded past.

And the Quarter, at night when the dark fell down, providing a man was blessed or maybe cursed with rhythm in his heartbeat, was a sure enough paradise. Music pouring thick as cane juice out of almost any doorway—music so powerfully wonderful that it played up and down the bones of your backbone like it was a xylophone. It made a man want to dance no matter how long his years or how big his bunions.

Gideon Jones didn't rightly know just how old he was—but he knew for sure certain that he'd ankled along past that milepost they called "Prime." He had quite a lot of grizzle in his hair, twinges in his joints, and a stiffness in his fingers that kept him from making fancy music with a trumpet in a way that used to be a real caution to hear.

Time was, once upon a Bourbon Street, when folks had come from just about everywhere to listen to Gid Jones. It had been mighty fine standing on the platform with a big old spotlight hitting you sprang in the face like it was your own special sun. Faces staring up at you and the room filled up with layers of smoke of all colors like it was one of those fancy lady's drinks they called a *pousse-café.*

The nights and the years had slipped by swift and easy like a catfish going downriver with the current pushing on his tail. One morning, Gid looked in his shaving mirror and saw that the Gid Jones he had known had been gobbled up like an oyster, leaving an empty old shell behind.

He hadn't played much now in quite a long spell—but it was a real pleasure to know how many people still remembered him. Most of them were now white-haired and overweight—but they brought their children or grandchildren down to the Quarter, saying "You've never heard a trumpet played until you've heard Gideon Jones and his Goldie!"

So, come every evening, Gid gave Goldie a good polish. Then, with her battered case under his arm, he headed toward the Quarter. His wide nostrils drank up the smell of his ladylove, New Orleans—a voluptuous Creole girl, perfumed with jasmine, who lay on a muddy river bank eating a fish sandwich.

Some nights, if there was some old-timer in the crowd who recognized him, he was asked to come up on a band platform. It was almost like old times. The spotlight was just as hot and bright. The blur of ice-cube faces at all the tables was just as silent and listening. And Goldie's voice came out her bell as strong and timeless as Old Man River—saying things that had never been said before and would never be said again. Gid once heard a young fellow say to his girl, "Boy! That old guy may look like the devil but he plays like an angel!" Gid took it as a real compliment. He'd been born ugly—but it'd taken him a lot of years to really play trumpet.

On this particular evening, Gid made do with a supper out

of a can of beans, a paper bucket of ice cream, and a bottle of instant coffee. If he had known it was his going away supper he might have had something more fancy—maybe some mustard sardines, a hunk of pecan pie, and a small glass of wine to give him courage on the trip.

After washing up his few dishes, Gid put Goldie's case under his arm, clumped down the stairs, and aimed his big old feet toward the Quarter. It was a real pretty night, almost too warm for January. Where did that last year go for it to be January again? Before long it'd be time for Mardi Gras!

Seems as though he'd seen maybe a million Mardi Gras— and which year was it that man from New York or Chicago or someplace else had offered him and Goldie big money to come away from New Orleans and play for folks up north or east or west?

It didn't really matter—but Gid stopped and leaned against a building to let his mind wander back into a maze of old Mardi Gras. His eyes closed and his head dropped. Then his knees bent and he slid down the wall—coming to rest in a sitting position on the sidewalk.

Children, playing under a streetlamp, thought he was just another old man who had had too much to drink and had gone to sleep. A few minutes passed and a young punk with loose hair and tight pants came along.

Making sure that he was unobserved, the punk bent down and swiftly went through Gid's pockets. It wasn't much of a haul. Fifty-two cents in loose change, some keys, a rabbit's foot and a chewed-on pencil. Still—there was the trumpet case. And pawnshops.

Goldie, who had lived with Gid Jones until she was a part

of him, knew she was being carried off by a strange hand. It has been said that inanimate objects cannot cry. But they do. Like Goldie, they cry on a note of such high desolation that it cannot be heard by the human ear.

Gid Jones opened his eyes when the great carrier broke through the barrier of morning mist on the rim of the universe. He'd been dreaming that he was a young hoss again—tooting horn for Cap'n Cabe Tollivar on the old Magnolia Blossom Showboat. Looking down at the Celestial City, he thought for half a moment that the Magnolia Blossom was coming in for a landing at New Orleans—but then he recalled that Cap'n Cabe and his showboat had been gone for many a year. Not only that but the Gates, which opened friendly-like at the top of some pretty and easy-climbing stairs, were a lot bigger and more elegantly wrought than any he'd ever seen around the Vieux Carré.

Gid was the last passenger to leave the carrier because he stayed behind to search everywhere for his horn-friend, Goldie. She was nowhere to be found. At last, he gave up—and feeling quite lost and naked without her case under his arm, he slowly and sadly followed his fellow travelers up the famous Stairs which led to the great Gates of the peerless Celestial City.

Awaiting him on the topmost step was his assigned guardian angel, Seraphita. Gid had been one of her favorite clients—and, if she had ever been questioned by her superiors, she would have to admit that she had given him more than his fair share of her protection. She had grown to love New Orleans and it had been most exciting to hover over Bourbon Street.

Often, in some ink-black bar, when Gid and Goldie had been on the platform making music, her wings had been set a-dancing—and she had flown back and forth through the spotlight's beam. People, seeing her shadow, had thought it was the shadow of a moth. Due to an alcoholic haze, their eyes had seen an angel caterpillar instead of an angel guardian.

Observing Gid's unhappy face, Seraphita assumed her most comforting heavenside manner and hurried to meet him.

"Good evening and welcome to the Celestial City, Mr. Jones!" she called. "My name is Seraphita—and quite unknown to you, we are very old and good friends! I do hope you had a pleasant journey!"

"Thank you, ma'am," Gid replied morosely. "I guess it was all right because I must have slept all the way. I don't even remember leaving or any scenery we passed along the way."

"It there anything troubling you, Mr. Jones? You appear to be so—," Seraphita searched her memory for a down-to-levee colloquialism, "so—so unbejoyful!"

"Well—now I don't want to point a finger at nobody I rode with and say they was light-fingered—," Gid was apologetic but firm, "but I do happen to be missing a trumpet in a trumpet case."

"Oh, that's easily explained, Mr. Jones! They were left behind. You see, the carriers are not allowed to carry any personal belongings."

"Left behind!" Gid was aghast. "Right there on the street? That's a terrible careless way to treat a man's property. Goldie's too fine a trumpet to use that way!"

"We'll find you another one, Mr. Jones!" Seraphita put a

consoling hand on his arm. "There's a trumpet shop on the Avenue of Adoration that has some perfectly beautiful instruments. Why, the other day, I saw one in the window that was exactly like the one Joshua had at the siege of Jericho! Chances are they'll have one for you that's even better and more to your liking than Goldie!"

"Begging your pardon, ma'am—there is no trumpet nowhere that is nohow better than her!"

"I shouldn't have said better—that was just an unfortunate slip of my silly tongue, Mr. Jones!" Seraphita chewed nervously on a wingtip. "What I meant to say was that I'm sure we'll find a nice instrument that may be just about as good as! Now—for the time being, don't you worry your head about it because I must get you settled. Ever since I learned you were coming, I've been giving the matter a great deal of thought—and I do believe I've found a place that you're just going to love! If you'll come with me, Mr. Jones—"

Seraphita guided Gid through the massive Gates, where he was warmly greeted by Senior Saint Peter and given his small, golden souvenir gate key. Then, side by side, he and Seraphita started across the green and beautiful Plaza of Eternity.

This evening, as on every evening, people had come in from every part of the vast Celestial City to walk its winding, flower-bordered paths and to sit on its many benches. At this hour, on any other night, the Plaza was filled with voices speaking in many tongues of remembered times and people and places—a river of sound with sudden and merry ripples of laughter that flowed from the famed Gates to encircling Eden Way. But on this particular nightfall, the great park in the oldest part of the City was as quiet as a whisper-locked lake.

Well... perhaps not that quiet. Dysmas, the thief, shifted his weight from one leg to the other and his right knee cracked like a broken stick. And Miss Angela Barnworth, holding Old Cat in her arms, gave a tremendous sneeze when his lashing tail tickled her nose. And Captain Noah stepped on Mrs. Noah's foot and that lady gave him such a dig in the ribs with her elbow that he said 'Whoosh!' And the shoes of Otto Schnitter, the school bus driver, squeaked like an ungreased chariot wheel when he tiptoed to a better spot. And Sukie, who was there with the other cherubs from Angels' Aide, was shaken with the loudest attack of hiccoughs ever heard in the Celestial City.

But there was an expectant silence—even Sek and his Shinar friends stood open-mouthed and mute, as though they'd never been associated with the Tower of Babel—and every head was lifted and every eye searched the dark sky.

"What's everybody looking for?" asked Gid politely as Seraphita steered him across crowded Eden Way and into the broad Avenue of Compassion.

"This is the Night of the Fireflies!" replied his companion. "It's a very special holiday—and although it's been celebrated for goodness knows how many centuries, everyone still 'ohs' and 'ahs' as though the spectacle was occurring for the very first time."

"Something better than a Mardi Gras parade?" Gid inquired.

"Oh, much better! Look up there, Mr. Jones—," Seraphita lifted her arm and pointed to the far horizon where the night sky met the Elysian Fields.

Gid squinnied up his eyes but he couldn't see anything to

get excited about—just a few bitsy bright sparks. But as he watched, the few became a multitude—and the multitude became a legion—and the legion became a host as untold millions of fireflies rose from the Fields of Elysian!

Glowing, gleaming, glittering, they soon covered the whole night sky and tented the great Celestial City with golden lace—delicate, exquisite lace, which changed in the wink of an eye from one intricate pattern to another.

"Well, now—," said the awed Gid, "that's really something to see. Tell me—how come them glowbugs got a special night all for themselves?"

"It's a lovely but long story, Mr. Jones—and someday, when you wander around the Plaza, you can go into the Library of the Archangels and read it." Seraphita seized his arm and, resembling a small, busy tug shepherding a reluctant ocean liner, urged him along the Avenue of Compassion. "You'll find it in a book called *Legends of the Early Dawn.* Shard, the Proprietor's chariotmaster during the creation period, is the author."

"Yes, ma'am," said Gid. "Trouble is, I don't read so good."

"Oh... Well—according to Shard—there was once an old prophet who lived down on Earth when it was almost brand, spanking new. The Proprietor thought very highly of this graybeard—because, unlike other members of his tribe, he neither worshipped graven images nor took part in orgies. Feeling that He should reveal Himself to this worthy man, the Proprietor commanded Shard to drive Him down to earth so that He could speak with the prophet."

"Wowee!" breathed Gid. "You know what I would've

done if that Proprietor had come down to New Orleans to speak to me? I would've fainted dead away."

"That's exactly what the old prophet did," said Seraphita. "He toppled like a felled tree and froze in a deep trance. 'Oh, the poor man!' said the Proprietor with great sympathy. 'Do you think, Shard, that it is quite fair to burden such a frail and fear-cracked vessel with such a tremendous truth?'

"'He's the best of the lot, Sir,' answered Shard. 'Another one, even half as good, might not come along for a couple of centuries.'

"'I know,' the Proprietor sighed. 'These earthlings are a disreputable and disgraceful lot and only a Father could love them.' Then, shaking His head sadly, He bent and planted a precious seed of knowledge deep in the memory of the unconscious prophet.

"The next morning, when the graybeard awakened and discovered the seed, his whole anatomy started to quake and quiver in terror.

"'Oh Great Visitor of the Night!' he sobbed, 'You have brought me to ruin! I dwell with a fierce and cruel tribe that merely tolerates me because I call myself a prophet! But I am not a prophet! I am just a poor old man who has a secret throbbing in a big toe which allows him to foretell rain! If I whisper a word of this knowledge to the tribe it may mean my death!'

"All the day long, the panic-stricken man sat in his cave— and as the hours passed, the seed grew and grew in his head until there was no more room for panic. At nightfall, when the tribe gathered around the leaping fire, he came out of his cave and raised his voice.

"'Hark to me!' he shouted. 'I have great tidings to impart! This world of ours was created by God! He is our Father and we are His children! If we put our trust in Him, He will help and protect us!'

"'Silly old goat!' laughed a tribesman. 'Where—,' he demanded, 'Where does this wonderful God dwell?'

"'Up there!' cried the prophet, pointing upward, 'Up there—beyond the stars!'

"'Beyond the stars!' hooted another tribesman. 'That is beyond the reach of any man's imagination!'

"'Do you take us for fools?' the chief of the tribe spat scornfully. 'A star is farther away than forever! If we shouted for help, how could the ear of such a far-off God hear us?'

"'Let us see if this Great One can hear you, old graybeard!' guffawed a burly member, picking up a stout club. 'Scream your loudest and we will find out if your voice can reach beyond the stars!'

"And they beat him and stoned him and the old man's feeble cries seemed to rise no higher than the treetops.

"It has been said that the ear of the Proprietor can hear the smallest spider tiptoe across its soft, silky web in the farthest and most remote part of His infinite domain. In answer to the old prophet's cries, He seized a great golden lightning bolt and crumbled it in His hands! He gave each minute shining fragment the breath of life and the gift of wings! Then He cast these specks of living light upon earth's summer night— where they flew about like tiny glowing stars—a whole sky of stars within reach of a child's hand!

"And when the tribe saw these stars, it was overcome with dread! It threw itself on the ground and covered its collective head in abject fear! The stars had come down to earth and the mighty God, who dwelt just beyond them, must be close with His vengeance!

"And they implored the old prophet to protect and save them—promising to be forever kind and friendly and considerate—vowing to travel far and wide and tell of God.

"To the Proprietor's surprise, the tribe kept its word. Like fireflies, the members carried the bright spark of knowledge to far campfires—and peace and goodwill spread slowly over the Proprietor's new little planet Earth."

"That's a mighty nice story," said Gid Jones as he and Seraphita crossed the last Millennium Circle. "Is it true, ma'am?"

"Of course it's true!" His guardian tried to control a slight touch of asperity in her voice as she answered this inane question—reminding herself that all newcomers to Celestial City seemed to have a broad streak of doubting Thomas running through their comprehension when confronted by the most minor and run of the mill miracle. "I can assure you that if it wasn't an absolute verity, it wouldn't be in the Library of the Archangels."

A capful of wind brought the winy smell of seaweed and salt water to Gid's nose—and his ears heard the soft chug-a-lug of wave-washed pilings as he and Seraphita came to an immense harbor with wharves stretching farther than any eye could see.

"Evenin', Miss Seraphita, ma'am!" roared a foghorn voice from a ship that was ghosting by to its berth in Big Fisherman Bight.

"Good evening to you, Captain!" she called. "That—,"

she explained to Gid, "is our Captain Vanderdecken and his Flying Dutchman. There must have been a bad storm off the Banks and he's brought in that poor fishing smack."

"That's a pretty beat up boat," remarked Gid.

"Just wait until it drops anchor," smiled Seraphita. "It will be as seaworthy and yare as it was on the first day it sailed—and its captain and crew as strong and handsome. This, Mr. Jones, is Fiddlers' Green. It's very much like your waterfront in New Orleans—only it's safer—and kindlier. Near here is the place I have in mind for you. It's on Bayou Creole. If you'll follow me, please—"

They went along a cobbled way that was lined with shops that held everything that any ship, large or small, might need; chain, lanterns, sail cloth, paint, spars, brass polish, whistles, belaying pins, sweeps, hammocks, bilge pumps, galley stoves, barometers, deadeyes, oakum, sextants, valves, and bins and bins of stuff that would be of no use to anyone unless he was a sailor.

A sign on a starlamp post directed the way to Bayou Creole—and Gid tagged along after Seraphita through a tunnel of live oaks. And somewhere, just like back in New Orleans, a sweet jasmine bush was cuddling up with the night and saturating its black evening clothes with a heady perfume.

They came out of the tunnel of great, moss-hung trees into bright moonlight—and there, before Gid's eyes, was the waterfront that his young manhood remembered. Tied up, all in a row, was every packet boat—side-wheeler or stern-wheeler—that had ever plied Big Miss. Stately river queens in whiter-than-white dresses with row on row of gingerbread ruffles.

Every stateroom of every packet was lighted and through

the open doorways of their saloons, Gid could see the shadowy figures of dancers moving to the songs and the rhythms of another day.

Only a few steps away was the gangplank of a floating palace. If he wasn't dreaming, it was the Magnolia Blossom Showboat. He'd known every inch of that old Blossom way back when he and his trumpet Goldie were just getting the hang of each other. A lot of water had gone down river since then—but he still thought of the Blossom as his first real home.

"Are you satisfied, Mr. Jones?" asked Seraphita.

"Yes, ma'am, I am," said Gid.

"Then I'll leave you. Goodnight, Mr. Jones."

"Goodnight, ma'am. And thank you kindly."

Gid waited until her footsteps had died out down the tree tunnel and then he ran to the gangplank of the Magnolia Blossom.

"Cap'n Cabe Tollivar!" he called. "Cap'n Cabe—are you there?"

"Who's that wantin' Cap'n Tollivar?" roared a familiar voice—and out from the door to the ticket booth bustled a little man wearing a cap that had more gold braid than an admiral's. His cheeks were ripe Jonathan apples nestled in the shredded white tissue paper of his luxuriant side whiskers. "The next performance ain't until... why, Gid! Gid Jones, as I live and breathe!" He trotted down the gangplank on his short legs. "I knew you was comin' but I didn't know just when!" He embraced Gid as though he were a long lost prodigal returning to the fold. "The girls have been fixin' up a stateroom for you—new curtains and all kind of fancy do-dads until it looks like the boudoir of a Tchoupitoulas Street flossy!"

"Girls?" asked Gid. "What girls?"

"What girls, he asks me!" laughed Cap'n Cabe. "The girls of the company, of course! Vivienne and Beth-Ann and Juliet and Doreen!"

"They're all here?"

"Certainly they're all here! If they weren't, how could I give a show every night!" He turned to the showboat and his voice woke the echoes of Bayou Creole. "Look alive, folks! Come along down here an' see what I got!"

A moment passed—and then all the well-known figures came down the gangplank to greet him. The first was blonde and ethereal Vivienne Lovely, the leading lady, who had been the secret love of every male heart hidden beneath a sweat-stained workshirt from Cincy Town to the Crescent City; the second was the elegant Beau Ravenford, her husband and leading man, who had—in their romantic dreams—kissed the longing lips of ten thousand amorous maidens in rustic cabins and bayou houseboats.

Following them came the dark and sinuous Doreen Collingwood—and her husband, the fierce and black mustachioed Dirk Darwin. On stage, as villain and villainess, they had appeared as evil as a pair of water moccasins—but off-stage, they had been as devoted and domestic as Mama and Papa Swamprabbit.

Then, running with a great display of petticoats and red garters to give Gid a hoyden's bear hug, was Beth-Ann Manners, the impish soubrette—and she was pushed aside by the excited Jacques Champagne, the dashing juvenile, who forgot his cultivated English drawing room accent and lapsed into Cajun.

J. Fennimore Duncan and Juliet Marchbanks were warm but more restrained in their greeting, as befitted a couple who played character parts—but Juliet gave Gid's cheek a motherly pat and said it was plain to see that he hadn't been eating properly, too many canned beans and too much ice cream and instant coffee—and J. Fennimore puffed on his pipe and advised, in a stern, fatherly voice, that Gid settle down on the Magnolia Blossom before he ruined his health.

Then, rising over the bedlam of voices and warm laughter of all the showboat thespians, came the loud bray that heralds a true Toby comedian. Down the gangplank, leading Big Bertha, the cook, and Slowpoke, Sooner, and Jellybones, the crew— came Happy Hogan. Suspenders held up his too short, over-sized pantaloons. His shirt, a green and white checkerboard, was decorated with an enormous bow tie of screaming red.

His freckled face creased in that ear-to-ear, zany grin that had delighted so many thousands, Happy Hogan pranced up to Gid and took his hand. Gid waited for an artful dig in the ribs from a foxy elbow and a familiar but timely quip that would make everyone scream with laughter and say "How does he think of such funny things!"

But Happy Hogan just stood and looked at Gid. The broad, brash grin folded in upon itself like a crushed accordion and became a child's mouth that trembled slightly in its intense desire to form the right words which all grownups could understand.

"How are you, Gid, boy," he said in a husky whisper. "Nice to see you. Right wonderful to have you home."

Later, lying in his bunk on the Magnolia Blossom, Gid thought back through the evening that had begun on a street corner in New Orleans. The Stairs. The Gates. The great Plaza of Eternity and walking out the Avenue of Compassion on the Night of the Fireflies. The grand feeling of finding old friends who remembered you kindly. And the shining beauty of the old Magnolia Showboat to prove that nothing good and loved is ever lost—but lives forever in Bayou Creole or someplace else.

"Three o'clock!" The faint cry came through the night from Fiddlers' Green, where a watch angel guarded the sleeping ships and crews. "Three o'clock on a fine, clear, celestial evening—and all's well!"

Yes, thought Gid, everything was elegantly well—except for Goldie. Maybe it was plumb silly to worry his head about a little old horn. Sighing, he went to sleep—and he dreamed that Goldie called out to him in her sweet, brassy voice—crying to him for help in her terrible grief and trouble. In the morning, every muscle ached from the miles he had run in his sleep to find her so that he could blow sweet nothings into her mouthpiece to comfort her.

The days were iridescent bubbles floating down an endless, tranquil stream. Gid found the trumpet shop on the Avenue of Adoration—and as Seraphita had assured him, it was filled with trumpets of every shape and size. He found one that in his opinion wasn't too bad—and the patient shopkeeper, who had endured Gid's glum tooting on a hundred of his best horns, told him that he had selected the finest instrument in his whole stock—and solid gold from mouthpiece to bell.

But its gold wasn't near as golden as Goldie's brass—and it couldn't cry up a haunting memory the way she could. This one could sing of glory, beauty, peace, goodwill and all the great wonders of the Celestial City—but it had never been to the levee country. It had never seen the loveliness of water hyacinths—or opened the oven door of morning where the rising sun was baking the night's fog and giving out all the smells it had gathered on the waterfront—or learned the music in a shanty girl's laughter in a new mail-order dress—or watched a white, longnecked bird making a nest in a sad old tree that was crying long mossy tears.

126

It had never hunted a job—or played slow and solemn on the way to a graveyard and fast and frisky coming back—or hitched a ride on a freight—or been tarnished by July's sweat—or had February's flu germs blown into it.

It had never sang out to courtyard windows to pretty please throw down a penny or a dime—or slept on a lumpy mattress with a herd of hungry bedbugs—or felt a drop of rain, a sliver of sleet, or a flake of snow. Its mouthpiece had never know the fragrance of barbecued ribs—or tasted turnip greens or black-eyed peas or cornbread or baked yams. It had never married a man for better or worse—and put up with his bunions, rheumatism, toothaches, constipation, body odor, and all the other unheavenly things that a human being might be heir to in his lifetime.

This new trumpet was a real beauty—and being solid gold, it must be worth a lot more than Goldie—but when it came to earthly things, its abysmal ignorance made Gid want to cry.

Still, it would have to do—and when it and Gid got together to entertain folks between the acts of an old melodrama at the Magnolia Blossom Showboat, it came out fair to middling. Leastways, they applauded and stamped their feet as though they thought the old fellow and his horn kind of tickled their ears.

Come nightfall, six days a week, people would meander down that tunnel of live oaks to the gangplank on Bayou Creole. They came from every part of the vast Celestial City to pay ten, twenty, or thirty blessings to see the same old plays done in the same old way. They hissed Dirk Darwin's fiendish skullduggery—wept over Vivienne Lovely's shining innocence—guffawed at Happy Hogan's clodhopper wit—and shouted with glee when virtue triumphed.

There was one man, Gid noticed, who came three-four times every week. He had sort of a dignified, saintly look as though he might be a deacon, maybe, of some church. Only he wasn't at all stiff or sanctimonious. He could laugh and applaud louder than anybody in the whole audience.

"Who—," Gid asked Cap'n Cabe, after several weeks of puzzlement, "who is that customer who comes around so regular?"

"Oh," said Cap'n Cabe, "that's Mister Genesius. Dotes on showfolk. He's their backer—or patron, if you want to use a fancy word. If I want a set of scenery—or new footlights—or maybe a special costume—I just speak my need in his ear. Next morning, there it is—compliments of Mister Genesius."

Time passed and down in New Orleans it was Mardi Gras again. In the Celestial City, the trees were big pompoms of spring blossoms and everybody was beginning to think about Easter.

On this particular noontime, Gid and Cap'n Cabe were stretched out on two bales on the levee at Bayou Creole. Somewhere, in the reeds up-bayou, some bullfrog had collected enough of his brethren to make a full bass tuba orchestra and it was whump-whumping in three-four time.

"This," said Gid, patting his bale, "is the softest cotton I ever laid me down on."

"T'aint cotton," yawned Cap'n Cabe, from his bale. "This here is baled cloud."

"Don't give me that." Gid stretched himself. "Nobody can grow cloud and bale it."

"It's the gospel truth." The captain crossed his heart and held up his right hand. "If you don't believe me, you go up yonder. There's acres and acres of plants looking just like a cottonfield—only the bolls are burstin' wide open with cloud."

"What's it used for?"

"Anything you want to use it for after it's spun and woven. Cherubs' robes for the children down at Angels' Aide— window curtains for Mr. and Mrs. Noah's Animal Shelter— seat covers for Otto Schnitter's school bus—sails for ships like the Flying Dutchman—all kinds of things."

"Well, I never." A shadow fell across Gid's face and he opened his eyes. A stranger, with a serious, deeply lined face, was looking down at him.

"I'm sorry to disturb you," said the stranger, "but I'm searching for Gideon Jones."

"That's me." Gid sat up, wondering if this might be a collector and Cap'n Cabe had forgotten to send the last blessing payment on the new trumpet. "Only most everybody just says 'Gid.'"

"My name is Joshua. I was talking with Mister Genesius down at the Plaza last evening. In his opinion, you are one of the finest trumpet players in the Celestial City. To quote him exactly, he said, 'Gid can blow up a storm.'"

"That was right kind of him." Gid's face broke in a pleased smile. "Tell me, Mr. Joshua—do you play trumpet and were you ever 'round a place called Jericho?"

"Yes, I do and was, Mr. Jones."

"A preacher I heard one time in Natchez told me—and these were his exact words— 'Joshua blowed down a wall.'"

"Well—a wall or a storm, they both need quite a bit of know-how, Gideon." Joshua put out his hand and Gid shook it. "Now—as to the purpose of my visit—how would you like to play for the sunrise service on Easter morning?"

"I'd like that fine." For another musician to offer an invitation to perform on such an important date made Gid feel very humble. "I'd be more than proud."

"Then we'll consider it settled. Your acceptance will be set down in today's report to the Proprietor. I'm sure He'll be pleased." With a bow and an airy wave of his hand, Joshua turned and strode off down the tunnel of live oaks.

"Gid, son!" spouted Cap'n Cabe, every hair of his side whiskers standing stiff and a-quiver like those on a cat's tail in a violent electrical storm. "This is the most stupendous thing that has ever happened to the old Magnolia Blossom Showboat! All those actors and singers and tooters and dancers who have come and gone on her stage! I've often wondered if I'd ever see one of their names giving a command performance for a president or maybe a crowned head of foreign parts! And now it's happened—only it's bigger than anything I ever dreamed! It ain't for just some measly king or queen or head of state—it's for the Proprietor—and the Proprietor's Son— and the Archangels—and the Patriarch Prophets—and the whole Celestial City on an Easter morning!"

When they heard the news, the other members of the showboat troupe were as excited as Cap'n Cabe.

"I don't think you fully realize how truly wonderful this is, Gideon," said J. Fennimore Duncan, the character man. "On earthly calendars, Easter is a red letter day—but in the Celestial City, it is golden.

"It is the gladdest, most joyful day in the whole year—and it seems even more so because of the quiet, hushed days that precede it. The great Gates at the top of the Stairs wear a shroud of black mourning cloth—and all movement in or out of the City is through a low, narrow door of blackest ebony piercing the towering Wall of Heaven.

"Even birds seem to whisper their singing during that week before Easter—and people walk about on tiptoe, speaking in whispers, as though the miracle of Easter was a fragile thing that could be frightened off by a sudden cry of a scuffed shoe.

"On the Street of Miracles, there is a small neat house that is occupied by the carpenter, Joseph, and his wife, Mary. On those few days before Easter, shawled women stand before it and weep silently. Mothers, of course—and as wives of butcher and baker and candlestick maker, they can know and share the grief of a carpenter's wife.

"On the Eve of Easter, not a single star is lighted and the night is as dark and impregnable as a sealed tomb.

"Every eye follows a single flickering spark that rises slowly to a great height. It is the lantern of the trumpet player—who, until this year, has always been Joshua—as he climbs to the top of the mighty Wall of Heaven.

"The player waits there—his eyes searching the black night. Suddenly, on the far horizon, there is a flash of light. The morning star has been rekindled by a distant watcher— the signal that the glory that is Easter morning is but a prayer-breadth beyond the rim of the universe.

"The trumpet is raised to the player's lips. Then, as the first ray of the Easter sun touches the top of the towering wall, the trumpet calls to all in the Celestial City to come and witness a great truth.

"The sun's light creeps downward, stone by stone, to the ponderous Gates—and as it reaches them, the mourning cloths fall away and the Gates swing wide and free—and the trumpet's brazen voice cries out, 'Believe! Oh, you of little faith—believe!'"

"I don't know." Gideon Jones shook his head. "I just don't know. I didn't know when I was asked that the trumpet part was so important. I'm just a little old boy from New Orleans— and I don't think I'm good enough."

"Joshua must think so or he wouldn't have asked you," said Vivienne Lovely, the leading lady.

"Good enough?" laughed Dirk Darwin, the villain. "Why, Gid, you're the tops!"

"Man—," chuckled Big Bertha, the cook, "if you can't make a horn speak out for Easter there ain't nobody can!"

"That's the livin', blowin' fact of the matter!" chimed in Slowpoke, Sooner, and Jellybones, the crew.

"Didn't you hear Joshua say that the Proprietor, Himself,

would be pleased?" demanded Cap'n Cabe. "And, if you think you ought to practice up a bit, you got near six weeks to do it!"

"Say you'll do it, Gid!" pleaded Beth-Ann Manners. "Please? Pretty please—?"

"Well—I'll think on it," said Gideon Jones. "I'll think on it real hard—that's the most I can promise."

The next day, Gid took his trumpet and drifted up yonder where Cap'n Cabe had said the cloud fields were located. As he came out from under a stand of yellow pine, he saw that Cap'n Cabe hadn't fed him a tall story. Bolls bursting white, the orderly rows of cloud plants seemed to stretch out farther than forever. He picked a strand and blew it off his fingers— and off it sailed like a baby sheep looking for a big fleecy mama cloud to nurse on.

In the shade of a red gum tree, a mule was dozing the day away. One long ear came half awake and turned reluctantly toward his approaching footsteps.

"I know you," said Gid. "Your name is Mule. That's the only name my pappy ever got around to giving you—just plain Mule." The sleepy animal opened one lazy eye to examine him. "Now don't make out you don't remember. Of course I was a heap smaller and you were a lot skinnier—but I'm Gid and you're Mule and I used to ride you to the crossroads store when I was sent for something we'd run out of."

Mule condescended to nuzzle him with a mouth that was all wet and drooly from some wonderful mule dream he'd interrupted.

"I was wondering—" Gid wiped off the slobber on Mule's neck, "I was wondering if you could tote me to some quiet

Gideon Jones practices the trumpet in the Vale of Valhalla.

place where I won't disturb folks. I got to get together with this trumpet and see if I can learn it something." He slid onto the animal's back and sat there, his long legs almost touching the ground. "Okay, Mule," he ordered. "Tote me."

Mule gave a sigh that stripped every boll on the nearest cloud plant. Then, after several violent switches of tail—evidently a necessary procedure to start the internal workings that operated the legs—off they went at a good steady pace.

After awhile the cloud plants thinned out—and they came to the wondrous and awe inspiring Vale of Valhalla. Here, with a force that makes the ground tremble as they fall an incredible distance to the rocks below, are the cataracts of rainbows. An eternal mist of many colors rises from the rocks and is carried to far-off worlds.

"You always was a smart one, Mule," said Gideon Jones. "This is a mighty fine place to learn a horn to speak up loud and clear." He slid off the mule and raised the trumpet to his lips—closing his eyes so that he couldn't see its cold, golden perfection—trying to imagine he was back in New Orleans with Goldie—and they were telling folks in her warm, brassy voice all about Easter.

Day after day, Gid and Mule crossed the cloud fields to the vale of the cataracts—and each night he returned with a visage so bleak and forbidding that no one on the Magnolia Blossom Showboat dared to question him.

On the Thursday night before Easter, he didn't return at all. There was no cause for worry, Cap'n Cabe insisted, because Gid, like everyone else, knew there were no performances on the showboat on this particular week.

They spent the evening brightly pretending that nothing

was wrong. Then, from Fiddlers' Green, came the cry of the distant watch angel.

"Twelve o'clock! Twelve o'clock on a fine, clear, celestial evening—and all's well!"

"All ain't well!" growled Cap'n Cabe. "Come on—follow me and let's find out what's happened to Gid!"

Under the light of the Proprietor's many moons which were burnished to a white brilliance to light the way of pilgrims everywhere, the showboat troupe went up Bayou Creole to the cloud fields. Here, the trail was easy to follow because Mule's feet, on many crossings, had made a well-defined path.

Coming to the Vale of Valhalla, they saw a distressed mule nuzzling a black rock—but on closer examination, it wasn't a rock, it was Gideon Jones. He was lying on the ground—and beside him was a trumpet of solid gold that would never play again. It had been battered and bent and stomped into shoddy, impotent junk.

"Gid!" cried the astounded Cap'n Cabe. "Gid, boy—what's wrong?"

"Go 'way. Just leave me alone!" He sat up and looked at them with a face that was a tragic mask of hopeless despair. "Didn't I say I wasn't good enough? Didn't I tell you all that I was just a little old New Orleans boy? If I was to practice a thousand years, I ain't got the lip to play a gold trumpet for nobody nowhere! You tell him that! You tell that Mr. Joshua I can't play on the big Wall and he's got to get himself another boy! Go on! Go on—just leave me alone and you go tell him that!"

Some hours later, a sad group was gathered in the auditorium of the Magnolia Blossom Showboat.

"I swear," croaked Cap'n Cabe, his side whiskers drooping like dewlaps on a basset hound, "I swear I don't know what to do."

"It seems to me," said Mister Genesius, who was sitting on the apron of the stage and swinging his legs, "that the problem is very simple. We must find Gid's old trumpet and give it to him."

"The one he called Goldie?" asked Happy Hogan. "But that must be down in New Orleans!"

"Exactly—but where in New Orleans is what we have to find out. That can be ascertained by careful perusal of the last Book of Time, reposing in the Library of the Archangels. The peregrinations of everybody and every thing is recorded—even so slight an item as a common pin from its first appearance to its final departure as a mote of rust. The exact whereabouts of this trumpet will most surely be noted."

"But—" said Cap'n Cabe, "supposing we do find out its location in New Orleans—how do we get it?"

"Very simple." Mister Genesius swung his legs. "We go down and get it—in the Magnolia Blossom Showboat."

"Very funny!" Sarcasm candied Cap'n Cabe's Adam's apple. "A showboat is a big, fat sitting duck—without paddlefeet or engines."

"It can't go anywhere without a tow boat," explained J. Fennimore Duncan.

"Of that, I am well aware," Mister Genesius said calmly. "I have thought on the matter—and I am sure that Captain Vanderdecken, if properly approached, will allow his Flying

Dutchman to be used for motive power."

"You are out of your saintly mind, if you don't mind my saying so," said Beau Ravenford, the leading man. "Captain Vanderdecken would never risk his precious Dutchman on such a voyage!"

"Faint heart never won a tug boat." Mister Genesius shrugged his shoulders. "Of course—if you don't care even an Annie Oakley about the trumpet and Easter and your friend, Gideon Jones—"

"All right!" Cap'n Cabe sighed. "*All right*! I don't guess there's any harm in asking. I'll take Happy Hogan with me to give him a few laughs to get him in a good humor—and Beau Ravenford to give class—and J. Fennimore Duncan to make a dignified pitch—"

"If you do that, Captain Vanderdecken will upstage you and the whole mission will be a turkey." Mister Genesius smiled and sunk his voice to a conspiratorial whisper. "Vanderdecken is a sailor—and what do sailors think about and dream about when plying the bounding main? I would suggest that the party be made up of you—wearing overalls if you like, because the Captain won't even notice—and Miss Vivienne Lovely, dressed in that blue frock she enhances in "Only An Orphan"—plus Miss Beth-Ann Manners in that frilly, bouncy creation which shows so much red stocking from "Poor But Honest." Now, time is short—so let's get this show on the high seas, so to speak! While you three are sugaring the salty Vanderdecken, the rest of us will hie ourselves to the Library of the Archangels to learn the exact whereabouts of Gideon's trumpet. Come on, everybody! Curtain! Action!"

Later, on the deck of the Flying Dutchman, Cap'n Cabe was feeling lower than the ship's submerged anchor. He had tried every trick in his talent trunk. He had orated. He had argued. He had pleaded. Beth-Ann had swung her soubrette curls and said 'pretty please' like a Lorelei. She had pirouetted and displayed enough red stocking to drive a sailor on the rocks.

"No," growled Captain Vanderdecken. "It is one crazy idea and I won't do it. Not a towboat is my beautiful Flying Dutchman! I will not dirty her paint or reputation on such a voyage! Till Doomsday from now, my answer is 'No'— 'No' on top of 'Positively!'"

138

"Dear Captain Vanderdecken—," until now, Vivienne Lovely had stood silent in the shadows—but now she came forward and the yellow light of the deck lamp illumined her slender, graceful figure. It also discovered every flake of gold in her blonde hair—lingered to caress the blue eyes, so wide, so clear, so innocent—and painted purple shadows under the cheekbones of the haunting, exquisite face that was remembered by old men in the legends they told when the day was hot, the beer warm, and the fishing tepid.

"We don't blame you for not wanting to risk your Flying Dutchman," said Vivienne Lovely. "She is your friend and you love her—just as we love our friend, Gideon Jones. But he and his trumpet mean nothing to you—and it was most presumptuous of us to try to shift our burden onto your shoulders. Do forgive us. We are so ashamed."

Tears welled in the blue eyes and rolled slowly down the delicate face—not the glycerin variety used by makeup artists to adorn the faces of lesser actresses, but the real, genuine saline kind that springs from a heartbroken lachrymal gland when a base villain has foreclosed a mortgage or a loved one has spent ten nights in a barroom.

"*Don't*!" Captain Vanderdecken's big, rough hands clutched the ship's rail. "Please—I beg you—don't cry! Tears from a beautiful woman I can't take! I go—you hear me? I take your showboat anywhere you want if you cry no more!" He strode off down the deck—his great voice bellowing and waking every sleeping sea gull in Big Fisherman Bight. "Olaf—Hans—Akim—Pierre—Mikhail—Giuseppe—all hands on deck! Turn out, you sea crabs! Cast off and heave the hook! We sail for Bayou Creole to pick up a tow for New Orleans!"

Mister Genesius and the other members of the showboat troupe were waiting for them on the Magnolia Blossom.

"Make ready the tow lines!" shouted Cap'n Cabe to Slowpoke, Sooner, and Jellybones as he ran up the gangplank. "Look sharp, now! Well—" he beamed a Halloween pumpkin smile on Genesius, "we've done our part and got the Dutchman! Have you found out what happened to Gid's trumpet?"

"We have, indeed," replied Mister Genesius.

"It was taken by a passing thief!" The character woman, Juliet Marchbanks sniffed her scorn.

"A despicable bit of knavery!" Dirk Darwin twirled his villain's mustache. "Purloining a musical instrument from a man who'd gone into a bit of a drowse on a street corner while awaiting a Celestial City carrier!"

"The thief took Gid's trumpet down to that hock-shop where I used to leave my overcoat in pawn for the summer!"

said Jacques Champagne in the light, cheerful voice prescribed by talent agents for juvenile men. "But that pawn-broker is a suspicious old octopus! He demanded proof of ownership—and then got on the telephone to the cops to find out if a trumpet had been reported stolen!"

"When the shopkeeper was occupied with his inquiry to the local constabulary—," J. Fennimore Duncan had confounded many a hash-house by asking if it had kippers or Yorkshire pudding on the menu— "this latter-day Fagin took off at a rapid pace and secreted himself in the passing throng!"

"Look!" snarled Cap'n Cabe. "I'm not interested in a minute-by-minute, inch-by-inch account! All I want to know is this—where is the trumpet right now?"

"We're coming to that." Mister Genesius smiled as though he were very much pleased with himself. "I do think you'll be surprised, Cap'n Cabe."

"Supposin' you was a thief, Cap'n Cabe—" Happy Hogan gave a hitch to his country-boy galluses, "what would you do with a hot trumpet that was too hot to handle?"

"Don't ask me riddles! Just tell me!"

"The thief went down to the river," said Juliet Marchbanks.

"He got on a ferry boat," continued Dirk Darwin.

"He waited, like a fearful rodent, until the craft reached midstream," added J. Fennimore Duncan.

"Then," said Jacques Champagne, "he dropped the trumpet and case over the rail."

"*What?*" exploded Cap'n Cabe. "*Do you mean to stand there and tell me—!*"

"Now don't excite yourself, Cap'n!" Mister Genesius held

up a restraining hand. I assure you that Gid's trumpet is safe and sound—right there on the bottom of the Mississippi."

"It might as well be in Gehenna! We ain't deep-sea divers and the girls ain't mermaids!"

"I have drawn a map which shows its exact location—depth, latitude, and longitude."

"Do you think Old Miss gives a ding-dang about a map? I know that river better than a man knows his wife's face! I know her current, mud, and general cussedness! How—in the name of all creation—do you aim to find anything as small as a trumpet case and fish it out?"

141

"I believe," said Mister Genesius mildly, "that the approved method for locating any underwater object is grappling. When we are successful, we will send down a swimmer to bring the trumpet and case to the surface."

"Oh, no," groaned Cap'n Cabe. "I'm not really standing here and getting sick to my stomach from all this drivel and balderdash. Tell me, somebody, that I'm sound asleep in my bunk and having a nightmare—"

"I would suggest, Cap'n," Mister Genesius became very stern and efficient, "that you refrain from guttural self-pity and get the Magnolia Blossom on her way to New Orleans. The distance is great and time and tide wait for no showboat."

"Tow lines all set!" called Slowpoke. "What now?"

"Cast off!" bawled Genesius.

At this moment, Big Bertha, the cook, who doubled as the calliope player and had always been proud of her reputation as the loudest and most indefatigable horse-piano player on the river, hit a deafening chord and then leaped into a lively and sonorous version of "O, Dem Golden Slippers."

"Shut that thing off!" shouted Cap'n Cabe.

"Good for the morale! Louder, Bertha!" commanded Mister Genesius.

It was also good for tumbling people out of their beds. It was estimated that half the Celestial City came running to Fiddlers' Green. Most people arrived too late to see the Flying Dutchman ghost out of Bayou Creole with the Magnolia Blossom in tow—and then, with all sails set, begin the voyage to recover the trumpet of Gideon Jones.

The Proprietor wasn't there—but from His cloudtop tower He watched the two ships, no larger than children's toys on the vast ocean of night, disappear from sight. A sudden moisture touched His eyes—and then He sent a swift messenger to The Stables on Eden Lane which lies in the eternal shade of the Wall of Heaven. The messenger was to ask Shard, His chariot driver of olden days, to come to Him.

It was shortly after two o'clock in the morning, central standard time, when a lean, tick-eared hound dog, sleeping under the rickety porch of a shack in St. Bernard Parish, raised his head from his paw-pillow. He rose and padded the few yards to the bank of Big Miss.

His nose tested the wind's breath for any strange smell while his eyes searched the river. After a few moments, he decided that neither friend nor foe neither moved nor smelled on this clear, starry night.

He was about to sit down and scratch an ever-hungry flea which had awakened from a sweet dream of living on a fat, city-bred poodle. The scratch was never consummated. The hound's foot dropped to the ground and alarm stiffened every muscle and raised every hair on his backbone. Two patches of river mist were moving swiftly up the river. The hound, trembling in every limb, threw back his head and howled with all his hound might.

At two twenty-one, central standard time, the banana boat Estrellita, outward bound after discharging cargo at New Orleans, was coasting down channel. Suddenly the helmsman muttered a fearsome oath and spun the wheel to starboard.

"Whassa matter—you go *loco*?" The startled second mate grabbed the wheel from his hands.

"That fog comin' up-river!" The helmsman pointed a shaking hand. "There's somethin' in it! I swear I saw a light!"

"Davy Jones' bicycle lamp, maybe? You gotta stop drinkin' that stuff!" sneered the mate. "That ain't nothin' but river mist!"

At this instant, a foghorn voice ripsawed its way through the leading patch of thick mist.

"Avast, ye banana bucket lubbers! To navigate, they teach you in a putt-putt on a millpond? Shove off, ye blasted galley stokers—or into your bilge I knock your binnacle!"

The second mate fell in a dead faint and the helmsman leaped over the rail and into the tawny waters of Big Miss. The Estrellita, with no hand on her wheel to comfort and guide her, ran erratically down-river until she met an oil tanker—and, like a motherless child, threw herself on its broad, maternal bosom.

At three o'clock in the morning, central standard time, Mister Genesius pulled up the grappling hook for the three hundred and twenty-second time.

"What have we now?" asked Dirk Darwin, the points of

his villain's mustache slightly blunted from weariness.

"Another rubber boot."

"That makes ten of 'em," said Cap'n Cabe morosely. "Another hour of this foolishness and we'll have enough boots to outfit a centipede to go trout fishing!"

"But we must be getting close to the trumpet, Cap'n Cabe!" protested Vivienne Lovely. "Just see all the things we've salvaged!"

"Tires, bedsprings, chamber-pots—," the husky contralto of Doreen Collingwood, the dark temptress of the Magnolia Blossom, made these items worth a king's ransom— "wagon wheels, horse collars, and a bear trap!"

"Garbage pails, bird cages, kitchen sinks!" Beth-Ann Manners was up to her red garters in water-soaked, rusted and battered loot which had been reclaimed from the muddy bed of Big Miss. "Wine casks, oil drums, coal scuttles, an iron skillet, and a barber chair!"

"A Dutch door, a baby carriage, a rabbit hutch, and a round dozen of mail boxes, old boy!" said J. Fennimore Duncan, the character man. "If we keep a stiff upper lip, we'll muddle through to success. I regard that outhouse door with the four-leaf clover cut-out as an excellent omen!"

"There's not one chance in a hundred million of hooking that case and trumpet an' you know it!" snapped Cap'n Cabe. "We might as well face the fact that this whole thing was a harebrained scheme of a bunch of nitwits." He looked at the circle of sad faces. "And I'm just as much a nitwit as anybody. I had real hopes... but grieving and crying ain't going to change things. Let's hail the Flying Dutchman and tell it to tow us back to Bayou Creole where we belong."

"Cap'n Cabe! Cap'n Cabe!" Slowpoke's feet pounded the deck. "They's a storm comin' an' Cap'n Vanderdecken's pullin' us over to shore!"

"Storm?" scoffed Cap'n Cabe. "The stars are full out and there ain't a cloud in the sky!"

"But look yonder—up Natchez-way, Cap'n!"

The night, an inverted, star-spangled teacup, was cracked on its northern rim by thin slivers of white flame. A great bull of a storm was loose in the night's china shop and growling distant thunder.

"Quick!" shouted Cap'n Cabe. "Throw all this river junk overboard and get the Magnolia Blossom ship-shape—this is going to be a real lollypaloozer!"

By the time the Flying Dutchman and the Magnolia Blossom arrived at the lee shore, the flashes were so brilliant, incessant, and imminent that they blinded the eyes of the frightened thespians. Thunder, so loud, so near, so menacing, shook every piece of glass and wood and metal on the two ships and they responded with terrified tinkles and groans and twangs.

Then—at the moment when eyes and ears could bear no more—the thunder and lightning ceased and the night became as dark as the belly of Jonah's whale and as silent as the pillar of salt that had been Lot's wife.

"Well, I never!" said Cap'n Cabe. "In all my years on this here river, I never seen such—"

"Captain Caleb Tollivar?" called a voice from the river bank.

"Speaking!" answered Cap'n Cabe. "What would you be wanting?"

"Is this the Magnolia Blossom Showboat?" Into view plodded a tall man with a fiery eye, a wind-whipped stork's nest of white hair, and a beard as large and as white as a double damask dinner napkin. Although clad in an over-sized and much rumpled nightgown, he still maintained great dignity and authority. "And is this the place on the river that hides the trumpet of Gideon Jones?"

"The answer is 'yes' to both questions," said Cap'n Cabe. "And now I got a couple. Why? and Who are you?"

"I would take it as a great favor if you would refrain from wasting what still remains of the night with unnecessary small talk!" the oldster replied testily. "Now—if you will pardon me—" He walked down to the water's edge and looked out at the muddy river. Then, raising his head, he addressed the stars in a deep, powerful voice:

"Sir?... Most exalted and omnipotent Sir? I want You to know that I'm not complaining—as You are well aware, I was willing, nay, eager, to obey Your slightest wish during my one hundred and twenty year residence on this trifling planet. Still—even You, in Your great wisdom—must surely admit that it is just a bit... well—shall we say uncharitable?— to ask a man of my extreme age and high position in Your Celestial City to exert himself at this unseemly hour and in this undignified manner? Really, Sir—to cast me among mountebanks to aid in the recovery of a common brass trumpet!

"I do, however, wish to lodge a complaint against Your chariot driver, Shard! He is a muscle-bound oaf and as crazy as a moonstruck camel! I was sound asleep in my house, a gift from You some thousands of years ago, in Beulah Meadow—

and dreaming of the perfect rose which I had just brought to flower in my garden—and which, out of respect for You, I had christened the 'Proprietor Rose.'

"I was aroused by a knocking at my door? Knocking? *Battering*! That brute of a Shard beat upon it with a gnarled fist until he cracked a panel! When I appeared, he tucked me under his arm as though I were a yammering, recalcitrant infant—carried me through my rose garden—and deposited me most urgently in Your chariot!

"That particular conveyance, let me say, is the most dreadful and harrowing means of transportation You ever created! Those enormous, pounding wheels tear the very firmament apart with crashing thunder! Those wild, gigantic steeds whose pounding hooves strike lightning bolts which sear the stars!

"And that madman—that Shard! He scorned the well-traveled road of our great carriers! At tremendous speed, we went rolling and rocking over paths that would scare the living gleam out of the most daring comet or meteoroid! Using such a vehicle and such a driver, my dear Proprietor, I am truly amazed that You were able to endure and complete creation!

"But, here I am, Your faithful servant still—albeit deafened, blinded, and bruised. From that lunatic Shard, I received the impression that You wish to repeat a miracle You and I performed in the long, long ago. If that is so—let us get on with it, most honored Proprietor. Very old and exceedingly weary, your servant, Moses, would like to go back to bed."

The patriarch, Moses, bent his big, white-thatched head—and into the beard that was larger than a double damask dinner napkin, he muttered some words in a tongue that was

147

Moses, aboard the Magnolia Blossom Showboat,
parts the Mississippi in search of Goldie.

strange to the troopers on the Magnolia Blossom. With fierce and burning eyes, he looked at Big Miss—the mighty Father of the Waters who had never acknowledged a master in all its miles or in all its years.

But, on this particular Easter Eve, it did. The patriarch, Moses, lifted his arms—and it parted as easily, as silently, and as completely as had the Red Sea, half-a-world away, for the passage of the Israelites.

Whooping and laughing and dancing and weeping silly tears, the members of the Magnolia Blossom Showboat went down into the bed of Big Miss. It was deep in thick, black mud—and after a few minutes, every thespian, even the dainty Vivienne Lovely, was covered from head to foot.

It was Mister Genesius who found the case. He opened it and held the trumpet, Goldie, over his head and yipped as loud as the most jubilant Comanche in the Celestial City's Happy Hunting Ground—and little Beth-Ann Manners, up to her red garters in ooze, threw her arms around him and gave him such a wet, muddy smack that Captain Vanderdecken scrambled aboard the Flying Dutchman—believing his beloved ship had split her foremast.

With all canvas set and a bone in her teeth, the Flying Dutchman brought the Magnolia Blossom home. As they came into the great, heavenlocked harbor of Fiddlers' Green, bells were rung and whistles were blown and foghorns were sounded and everybody agreed that no mariners had ever been given such a welcome.

Before dawn, on Easter morning, people came to the beautiful Plaza of Eternity from every part of the vast

149

Celestial City. Every eye followed the single flickering spark that rose slowly to an incredible height—and everyone knew it was the lantern of Gideon Jones, who was climbing to the top of the mighty Wall of Heaven.

Gid stood there with Goldie, the beloved, in his hand—his eyes searching the black night.

Suddenly, on the rim of the universe, there was a flash of light. The morning star had been rekindled by a distant watcher—the signal that the glory that is Easter morning was but a prayer-breath away.

150

Gid raised Goldie to his lips—and then, as the first ray of the Easter sun touched the top of the towering Wall, Goldie called out in her sweet brassy voice to all in the Celestial City—to all anywhere and everywhere—to come and witness a great truth.

As the sun's light crept downward, stone by stone, to the ponderous Gates—and Goldie, so brassy-wise instead of golden-foolish, went right on talking:

"Hey, there, all you nice, sad, wonderful folks down in New Orleans! Yes—and all you fine, grieving, beautiful people in Memphis and Cincinnati and Saint Louis and Cairo and any other little old place that knew Goldie and might be listening!

"Isn't it about time you stopped all this moaning and weeping and crying the blues? It was you, not the Proprietor, who created Death. Death is ugly and cold and mean—and the Proprietor doesn't truck with such. He only creates things of beauty—such as flowers and mountains and bird songs and frozen lace they call snowflakes.

"And hear me, all you heartsick, lovely people! The Proprietor got rid of Death a long, long time ago.

"Why, Death's been dead for two thousand years!

"Death died in a tomb near Calvary—didn't you know that?

"Don't try to bring Death back to life by watering him with your tears!

"Lift up your heads and sing, you sweet, sad, wonderful people—sing like you never sang before because it's Easter!"

V

It is safe to say that everyone in the Celestial City knows John T. Barnett. He lives in a palatial Victorian mansion out in Canaan Common. Passing cherubs delight in swinging on his gate, which is a large red and gold wheel from a circus bandwagon. The fountain in his front yard is another great attraction for the small fry. It is in the form of a clown—and, instead of water, it spouts pink lemonade.

Mr. Barnett came up to the Celestial City quite some time ago. It is said that earthly newspapers at the time devoted much space to his leave-taking. *Variety*, an amusement trade paper, had a full page lament addressed to "The Last of the Great Showmen."

After reading such dismal, dreary drivel, the many earthly friends and admirers of Mr. Barnett may have often thought of him through the years with much sorrow.

If this be so, we say unto you forget it forthwith! Mr. Barnett is hale, hearty, and happy and has taken a considerable step upward in his chosen profession. After all, it must be rated a pretty rare feather to stick in anyone's halo to rise from ownership of the Greatest Show on Earth to exalted entrepreneurship of the Grandest Show in the Universe.

Such an achievement is, of course, the consummate dream of every man who has ever spread a big rag over a vacant lot and waited for townspeople to step up to the ticket wagon. Ordinary men can never make the dream come true. John T. Barnett, however, is a stubborn man. Let a dream steal into his head and it'll find itself a gone gosling. Every brain cell in his head has the tenacity of any iron-jawed bulldog at Captain Noah's Ark on the Street of Miracles.

According to the saintly Peter's book, he came to the Celestial City on the fifth day of the earthly month of August. He had no inkling that this was get away day and he was headed for winter quarters. In fact, he had been busy counting tickets in the treasury wagon—and had been quite disgruntled when the carrier came for him.

Peter, although that had been a particularly busy summer afternoon with carriers arriving and departing every few seconds—heat prostrations, drownings, snake bites, and picnic food-poisonings—Peter says that he remembers Mr. Barnett because he stood out among the crowd of newcomers.

On that flight, Mister Barnett had been the last passenger to ascend the Stairs. He had stood by the steps of the great carrier for some time—the uncounted circus tickets still clutched in his big fist. With an appraising eye, he had

153

"This," he had remarked to Isui, "is certainly no tank town. The natives all look fat and prosperous, too. I imagine a man would have to hand out a lot of free tickets to saints and such—but, even so, a circus ought to do right well here."

"Why don't you try it?" Isui had answered. "The Proprietor allows people to do pretty much what they like."

"Well, I might just do that. Kitty? Here, Kitty—nice Kitty!" He had bent down to pat a cat that had come strolling aggressively down the exact center of the sidewalk. The cat had glared at him as though he were a silly gillie and walked on with its whiskers stiffly akimbo. "Not a very friendly animal, is he?"

"This is Canaan Common and that is Old Cat, Miss Angela Barnworth's heaven-spoiled darling," Isui had explained. "He's on his way to high tea at Captain Noah's Ark. He doesn't want to be late because Mrs. Noah serves him a bowl of yak cream."

"Really?" Mister Barnett had paused to eye his reflected image in a harp shop window. With finger and thumb he had sharpened the points of his mustache. "I used to have a pet yak. A runty little female that followed me everywhere because I hand-raised her with a nursing bottle. Her maw disowned her because her eyes were kind of funny. One was green and the other was blue."

"This ark-guest of Captain Noah's has eyes like that—and I believe Mrs. Noah calls it 'Pearly.'"

"That's her! That's my own yak!" Excitement or some highly personal emotion caused Mister Barnett's voice to crack. "I just can't hardly believe it—little old funny Pearly, after all these years. I'm going right down to that Ark and claim her!"

"You can do that first thing tomorrow morning," Isui had replied. "It's getting late and we've now arrived at our destination. There, below us, on the banks of the King Pole River, is the famous settlement which the Proprietor has named 'The Tanbark.' I hope it will please you, Mister Barnett."

John T. Barnett had stood awed and motionless to study the scene at his feet. It was, without the slightest doubt, the Big Lot multiplied by a trillion. White tents of every size and shape—endless rows of round mushrooms growing on endless acres of circus soil which had been fertilized by spilled soda pop, peanut shells, roustabout sweat, camel droppings, crushed popcorn and acrobat's rosin.

There were circus wagons and vans and cars—each so resplendent in its red and gold paint that it must have been painted on that very morning. Bright pennants danced and gaudy banners did the hootchy-kootchy as they were moved by a canvas-rippling breeze—and that same breeze, as bold as a spec girl in spangled tights, did an off-to-Buffalo up the hill to seduce Mister Barnett's nose with her pulse-racing perfume of acid-sweet sawdust.

All this, according to Guardian Angel Isui, had a strange effect on John T. Barnett. Without even a good-bye, he had trotted off down the hill toward The Tanbark on the King Pole River.

Isui stood there and watched until he had disappeared from sight on the endless midway. Then, smiling over a job well done, he had hastened off to the Down of Promise, where his house, his wife, his supper and a well earned rest awaited him. *Tomorrow*, he said to himself, *I will report to the Bureau of Guardian Angels that John T. Barnett has arrived and is content.*

At that moment, Isui's judgment of the situation was entirely correct. For a few days—even as much as a whole week—John T. Barnett was absolutely, positively content. He spent many happy hours shooting the breeze with acrobats, kinkers, hostlers, joeys, barkers, mule skinners, bull men, camel punks, and windjammers.

The only bit of tarnish on the tinsel was on the morning which followed his arrival in the Celestial City. He had set out very early to find Captain Noah's Ark and to claim Pearly, his yak.

He had walked up and down avenues, circled Millennium Circles and traversed innumerable lanes until he had been hopelessly lost. His crocodile hide boots had grilled his feet medium-rare—and the high crocodile tooth heels seemed to be gnawing the marrow from his leg bones.

Seeing a small, shady park, he had limped to a bench, eased off the boots, and waved his legs in the air to extinguish the fire in his toes. There had been a wellcurb nearby with a sign over it which had read "The Well of the Good Samaritan." A chattering child and a skinny, shifty-eyed man had just pulled up a brimming bucket of clear, cold water.

He had watched them pour this crystal elixir into a large pail—and he had instantly assumed that they were about to water some nearby elephant. His assumption had been wrong by a ton or more. The child had produced a small turtle from her apron pocket—and both had laughed merrily as the turtle did a belly whopper and went swimming about as gracefully as a muscular mackerel.

Filled with envy, Mister Barnett had watched this aquatic bliss for some minutes. He was then moved to say in his most plaintive voice—

"Pardon me—do you suppose your turtle would mind sharing that pail of water with my feet?"

"Oh, no—Herbie wouldn't mind at all!" said the child. "He has a very generous nature!"

"Indeed, yes," agreed the man as he had brought the pail and put it before Mister Barnett. "If anyone ever tries to tell you a turtle is selfish—don't you go believing it! Why, Herbie would give you the shell right off his back."

"Ahhhhhhh!" Mister Barnett had breathed as he eased his feet into the cool water. "This is heavenly! Truly heavenly!"

"My name's Sukie," the child had informed him as she bent over the pail and watched Herbie swim in and out between Barnett's spread toes. "I live at Angels' Aide."

"That's the famous cherub shelter on the Avenue of Compassion," her companion had added just as a bell sounded loudly from a distance. "And there's the school bell! Run, Sukie, or you'll be tardy again!"

"Oh, my goodness!" Sukie had seized Herbie and wrapped him in her handkerchief. As she had raced off across Second Millennium Circle, she had called over her shoulder—

"Don't forget to take back the pail before they notice it's gone, Dysmas!"

"I will—I will directly!" the man had cried. "I feel very bad about this," he had explained to Mister Barnett, "but I must ask you to remove your feet. It was on the back porch of Issac's house—and I borrowed it without his noticing. You may know him—he married Rebekah. Lovely couple. They met at a well outside the city of Nahor and it was a case of love at first sight. That was hundreds and hundreds of years ago, of course—but they insist on keeping their love new. They come to this well every eventide—she with her pitcher and he with his pail. They draw the water—and then they kiss and walk homeward."

"Well, love's a mystical thing," Mister Barnett had replied as he dried his feet. "Once you get stuck on it, it's worse than fly-paper. Tell me," he had demanded, "What would you think of a man who was more than a little fond of a yak?"

"I would consider him one of nature's gentlemen."

"You would?" Dysmas had nodded his head emphatically and crossed his heart. "Well, then—," the reassured Mister Barnett had continued, "There's this yak by the name of Pearly. Not much to look at. Real runty, you might say. Got eyes that don't match up. Some people have said she even stinks a little only I've never noticed it."

"Beauty should be observed by the eyes and not the nose," said Dysmas sympathetically. "That's an old proverb I just made up and which you can quote in the future, if you care to—"

"It's because of this yak that I'm sitting here worn to a frazzle. I was told that Pearly's been getting her board at Captain Noah's Ark—but I've walked this Celestial City long-wise and side-wise and I just can't seem to locate that blasted Street of Miracles!"

"Why, I can take you there in no time at all! It's just off Eden Way."

"I've been up and down Eden Way forty times and I

never found it."

"Ah!" Dysmas had chuckled as he handed Mister Barnett the crocodile hide boots. "You must be new here. Very new! Like all newcomers, you've still got a few doubts jingling around in some left-head pocket. To find it, you must believe in the Street of Miracles."

"Oh, I do!" Mister Barnett had stamped his feet into the boots. "If Pearly's there waiting for me after these twenty or more years, I really do believe in it!"

"Then come with me—" and together, with Dysmas carrying the pail, they had set a brisk pace down the Avenue of Adoration.

Between First and Second Millennium Circles, Dysmas had halted. Requesting silence from Mister Barnett by laying a finger on his lips, Dysmas had stolen down a small lane, keeping well below the hedges. He had placed the pail on a porch.

"I suppose," he said when he had rejoined Mister Barnett, "you think that a strange performance? Well—it's easily explained. I'm a thief." Mister Barnett's lifted eyebrows had brought a pleased smile. "Surprises you, doesn't it? I flatter myself that I'm the most famous thief in history. Yes, indeed—I've been told that they still talk about me down on earth. Of course, I haven't stolen anything for almost two thousand years—and I'd be pretty rusty if I didn't borrow things now and then when people aren't watching."

"Doesn't this borrowing bother the authorities?"

"Oh, yes! It bothers them dreadfully. And it infuriates them to know that by the time they complain to the Proprietor, I'll have returned whatever I've borrowed. Oh, now and then, when some Angel of the Peace is so angry that he's practically popping his halo, the Proprietor will turn to His Son and say, 'That black sheep of Yours is kicking up his heels again. You'd best find him and read him a good stiff parable.' And the Son goes searching for old Dysmas, who has strayed from the fold. When He finds me, He looks so sad and forlorn that it nearly breaks my heart. I weep and repent my evil ways—and He takes me in His arms and calls to the glowering Angels of the Peace— 'Come, rejoice with Me— for I have found the black sheep which was lost!'"

"I would say—" Mister Barnett had become slightly dizzy from negotiating the strange twists and miraculous turnings of the street they were now traveling, "I would say that I have the utmost admiration for a Man who defends black sheep. In my humble opinion, He could understand and sympathize with a man who's yak-minded."

"No question about it." Dysmas had stopped and pointed. "Well—there it is—Captain Noah's Ark! That lady in the front porch rocker is his wife. Come—I'll introduce you."

As they had crossed the Street of Miracles, Dysmas had nervously adjusted his robe and smoothed his hair. "Let me do all the talking," he had hissed. "We're very old friends and she likes and trusts me." Mister Barnett had nodded in answer. "Good morning, my dear Mrs. Noah!"

"Don't you come one step nearer, Dysmas," the lady had replied grimly without even turning her head. "I don't want you within arm's length of anything I got."

"Fear not, thou fair enchantress of the furious Flood—I have already accomplished my borrowing for the day!"

"Poof and poof-poof!" Mrs. Noah had snorted.

"Very well—to relieve your mind, I will sit upon my hands!" Dysmas had sat down on the curb with his hands under his bottom. "See? I am totally helpless. Now—the sole purpose of my visit is to help this gentleman. He desires to claim his pet yak."

"Yak?" Mrs. Noah had turned and appraised Mister Barnett—her eyes lingering on his boots as though she suspected that they might be carriers of crocodile rabies. "I suppose you're John T. Barnett?"

"Yes, ma'am—I am. My yak's name is Pearly."

"Uh," the lady had grunted. "I was told to be expecting you—but right up to now I've been kind of hoping you'd go and do something terrible to spoil your good record with the Recording Angels so's they'd cancel your reservation on the carrier. I've grown real partial to that little yak. Captain Noah!" she had called to the warm darkness of the Ark, "The man's here for Pearly!"

"Yes, Mother!" a voice had replied. "Coming right out!"

"When you live with a yak for a score of years, it seems like one of the family," Mrs. Noah had continued as she re-examined Mister Barnett. "But I guess she'll be glad to see you. To sort of prepare her, I took her out to The Tanbark Sunday last. As soon as we got nigh enough to hear the circus music and smell the sawdust, I was scared Pearly would go right out of her mind. She ran up the midway and into every tent—looking for you I guess. When she didn't find you, she just—well—drooped. It's a terrible, terrible thing to see an animal droop."

From deep within the old Ark had come the sound of four scampering feet. Then, out through the wide doorway, Pearly

*Old Cat watches as John T. Barnett and Pearly
are reunited at the Ark.*

had burst like a sob of joy from a bereaved breast when it is told it is bereaved no longer.

It was a reunion which will always be remembered on the winding Street of Miracles. At Angels' Aide, it is a bedtime story told to cherubs—although the story is known by heart by each cherub.

"And what did Mister Barnett say?" they ask the Grandmother in Charge— "And what did Pearly think?"— and "What did Dysmas do?"

"Oh, Dysmas!" the Grandmother smiles. "Well, you all know what a softy he is! He borrowed—borrowed, mind you—Mister Barnett's white top hat! He pushed it right down over his ears and eyes so that no one could see that such a wicked black sheep was crying!"

Everything would have been truly heavenly if Old Cat hadn't chosen that moment to appear for his usual tea-time snack.

Mister Barnett had thanked the Noahs for their long and tender care of Pearly. Hands had been shaken and good-byes had been said and Mister Barnett and Pearly had taken three steps away from the Ark's porch when Old Cat had entered the Street of Miracles from Eden Way.

In an instant, Old Cat's casual saunter had changed to a cavalry charge! That inferior biped—that crass individual who had tried to pat him only yesterday on the Avenue of Mercy— that scurvy scoundrel was about to steal Old Cat's sole source of yak cream!

Old Cat had attacked with every weapon in his catskin arsenal! The sounds of battle had risen to an ear-deafening crescendo—howls, screeches, wails, snarls, roars, grunts, bellows, growls, and heart-stopping wails!

The terrifying din of Old Cat's nine-lives-against-all-the-universe rage could be easily heard in the Plaza of Eternity—and Lud, Angel of the Peace, had come running. With some difficulty, he had separated the combatants.

"Now, then—," he had said as he massaged a bruise on his leg caused by Mister Barnett's boots—and wondered how he could explain the scratches on his face to his jealous wife, a sloe-eyed beauty who had been the favorite handmaiden of the Queen of Sheba. "Now, then—what is this unseemly ruction all about?"

"That cat—," Mister Barnett had pointed a shaking finger, "That blasted, philistinian alley cat attacked me!"

"Old Cat isn't really mean-tempered—he just spits before he thinks," Mrs. Noah had explained. "You see—I've been milking Pearly and skimming the cream off the top. I'm afraid he's become a yak cream addict. When he saw you leading Pearly away, his bile began to boil. A woman scorned isn't beans to Old Cat deprived."

"Well, for heavens sake," Mister Barnett had cried, "Tell that furred fiend that he can still have every drop that Pearly can manufacture! I've got no hankering for yak cream! Say that I give him an unbreakable guarantee! Tell him that if I should chance to get lost on some desert and I'm dying of thirst, I'll just have to sit and suffer because I don't even know how to work the combination on her milk supply!"

"Well, I'll try," Mrs. Noah had said doubtfully.

She had taken Old Cat on her lap and had talked long and softly into his laid-back, indignant ears. After a time, he had calmed down—except for an occasional baleful scowl in

166

Mister Barnett's direction and an embittered rumble deep in his solar plexus.

"I guess it's safe for you to go now," Mrs. Noah had whispered—and Mister Barnett, his head turned apprehensively over his shoulder, had led Pearly off down the Street of Miracles.

"Don't forget!" Mrs. Noah had called after him. "Bring her around every day so's I can milk her!"

"I will—I will!" Mister Barnett had lifted his hand to tip his white top hat to the lady and discovered that it was missing. *The heck with it*, he had said to himself, *I'm lucky to escape with my life and my yak!*

167

Things went smoothly after that. He, with Pearly ambling along beside him, roamed the vast Celestial City. They journeyed far and came upon subdivisions where the Proprietor was called by names that were alien to Mister Barnett's ears. They found people whose skins were golden yellow and cinnamon brown and raven black and rusty red. Pearly's favorite place was called Nirvana. Her instinct told her that in such a place her ancestors dwelt—and her nostrils flared to drink the smells of buttered teak and musk—and her ears stood tall to catch the music of camel bells.

And everywhere they went, people were smiling and obliging. Even Mister Barnett's landlady at his boarding-house at The Tanbark. When he had asked her, somewhat timorously, if she minded if he shared his room with Pearly, she had replied:

"I've got nothing against yaks. Not unless this one of yours plays the ukulele. I just can't stand that 'chunk-chunka-chunk.' Makes me think I'm back in the Hawaiian Show on the John Robinson Circus shaking a grass skirt."

After Mister Barnett had assured her that Pearly had no musical talent of any kind and had never even put a plugged nickel in a mechanical piano, she had said:

"You realize, naturally, that I gave you the single rate of one blessing on the room. If the yak's bunking in with you, I have to go up to the double rate of two blessings."

"Let's make it five blessings," had been his magnanimous answer. "That will cover extra towels and additional hot water. Yaks have been known to have a persistent perspiration problem." Pearly had lowered her head bashfully at this blatant disclosure of a hush-hush defect. "But this little yak is daintiness personified. Twice daily—morning and night—she takes her bubble bath."

Mister Barnett could well afford this seeming extravagance. On one of his first mornings in the Celestial City, he and Pearly had visited the massive building on Eden Way which housed the renowned Guardian and Trustful Angels. A young teller—schooled by some earthly bank to be efficient and by his new employers to be polite—had looked up Mister Barnett's account and had handed him his passbook.

Very sure in his mind that his savings could merely amount to a pittance, he had stuck the book in his pocket without looking at it—and he and Pearly had gone off to Fiddlers' Green to see all the ships in that famous, heaven-locked harbor.

Late that afternoon, as usual, Old Cat had slithered up out of nowhere to herd them back to the Ark for Pearly's milking. All the way to the Street of Miracles, he had walked on Mister Barnett's heels to hurry him up—and at every Millennium Circle crossing, he had growled out what could only be a whole series of tomcat expletives.

"Why don't you be cat enough to talk like a man?" the exasperated Mister Barnett had demanded. "If I could just decipher what you're saying, I could call an Angel of the Peace and have your mouth washed out with soap and water!"

Mrs. Noah had been waiting with her milking stool. Under the watchful eyes of Old Cat, she had gone right to work—her hands moving rhythmically to a ditty she had made up out of her own head:

"I know a yak and her name is Pearly,

Horns so cute and her hair so curly,

Swings her hips in a manner girly—

All each heavenly day!"

This sentimental twaddle, especially when Old Cat added his sandpaper-purr accompaniment, had disgusted Mister Barnett. He had taken his passbook from his pocket and had walked over to examine it by the light from the Ark's celebrated Dove Window. The figures set down in the book had shaken him to his crocodile boots. He had closed his eyes in disbelief—but when he opened them, the figures, unchanged, had still been there.

"It's not possible," Mister Barnett had murmured. "I couldn't have saved this much—why, I'm a wealthy man!"

As he had examined the many pages, he saw that every small kind deed he had ever done had been noted, written down and compound interest added by some meticulous accountant. Trifling, forgotten-in-a-moment deeds such as "Removing small sliver from a tiger's tail," "Paring painful corn on foot of limping ostrich," "Burping over-fed baby hippo," "Extracting large campaign button lodged an arm's length down a giraffe's throat," and "Pretending intense concern over a peewee cloud so that four youngsters could believe that they'd sneaked unnoticed under the sidewall and into the Big Top."

The milking done, he and Pearly had left the odorous old Ark and had made a slow way through the noisy end-of-the-celestial-day crowds toward their boardinghouse at The Tanbark. Pearly had immediately sensed that Mister Barnett's mind was intensely occupied with some profundity so she had walked by his side on tip-hoof.

At Third Millennium Circle, they had passed Otto Schnitter, the school bus driver. He had Luke, the Physician, by the arm and was telling the good doctor that today's smallest passenger must be immediately dosed with 'Luke's Efficacious Elixir For Homesickness.'

At Sixth Millennium Circle, their progress had been impeded momentarily by Sek and his Shinar friends. Each one had had a wheelbarrow loaded with stones or mortar—and shouting at each other, were headed down the Avenue of Justice toward the great Plaza of Eternity.

"What does that crazy crowd plan to do now?" someone had asked Solomon, the wise, who was watching all this hurly-burly with much amusement.

"They're off to build another Tower of Babel," he had replied. "their first one, from earth to heaven, was a frightful fiasco. They're sure they've got the problem licked. This time they're building it upside down from heaven to earth."

At Eighth Millennium Circle, Mister Barnett had stopped dead in his tracks in the very midst of the heavy go-home traffic between Canaan Common and Beulah Meadow. He had pulled the passbook out and had held it in front of Pearly's round loving eyes.

"You see those figures, Pearly? Those marks mean that you and me are rich as all get-out! You and me could live here in this Celestial City for a million or two million years and never even touch one blessing of the principal! Financially, you and me have got it made, Pearly—but who wants to sit around all that time doing nothing? Not you and not me! We'd get bored twiddling our fingers and hoofs—isn't that right?"

Pearly, to show that she was in complete agreement with anything that he might be saying, had kissed him from chin to forelock with a single swipe of her tongue.

"Now—you may have caught on to the fact that I've been absorbed in conscientious cogitation. I began by meditating over the fact that everybody here in this Celestial City seems to have some sort of job—and then I went a-pondering just what kind of work you and me might do. Well, Pearly—no matter how I cudgeled my brains, I couldn't think of one doggone thing. We're not towners like most of these Celestial City people—you and me are show-folk! 'Okie-dokie,' I said to myself. 'If a shoemaker sticks to his last—why shouldn't Pearly and me stick to canvas!' What would you say, Pearly, to you and me starting a circus?"

At the word "circus," Pearly's eyes had grown round as junior-sized millstones. It was a well remembered good time word that had all the breathless excitement of a ringmaster's whistle! It was a vagabond word returning to roost and it zipped down her ears, thumped on her eardrums and went 'round and around in her head as though it were a high school horse circling the center ring! In pure ecstasy, she had kissed Mister Barnett twice—once from chin to forelock and once from eyebrows to Adam's apple.

"You know, I was ready to bet my bottom blessing that you'd like the idea!" Mister Barnett had laughed as he pinched her dewlap. "Come on—let's get on to the boardinghouse. We got to get up early tomorrow morning and start framing our show!"

Side by side and horn in hand, Pearly and Mister Barnett had marched off toward The Tanbark—yak hoofs and crocodile boots thumping in time to a ditty which Mister Barnett had just made up, not out of his own head but out of his and Pearly's wishful thinking:

"We're off to start a circus!

The most wonderful circus of all!

A circus that is second to none

On any celestial ball!—"

A circus tent without a lot is a hen without a nest—and any smart impresario or canny farmer, before acquiring a spread of canvas or a pack of pullets, will provide a proper place for his planned property to squat.

To find the perfect location for what was to be the Grandest Show in the Universe had been the reason for all those before mentioned trips to the far places of the Celestial City.

Mister Barnett and Pearly had walked for ten long days. They had started out when the sun had lifted its tousled rays from beneath the eastern horizon—and had traveled until it pulled the western horizon over its sleepy head. Mister Barnett's shoulders slooped from the weight of accumulated despair. Pearly appeared to wear a yoke of doom, too heavy for any yak to bear.

On the tenth day plus one, they had plodded wearily homeward along Ninth Millennium Circle. Glancing to the left, Mister Barnett had seen a street which he thought might be a short cut.

It was named, according to a sign on the post which supported the starlamp, "Old Love Road"—a most appropriate name, Mister Barnett had decided after they had gone a way. The lawns were green calico dotted with round flower beds of old-fashioned flowers—and each roof had a brown, scalloped edge, as though it had been made from an old love letter or dance program, nibbled by the yellow teeth of time in some attic trunk.

Old Love Road had its own blend of perfume. Lilac blossoms and roasting chestnuts; vanilla cookies and sassafras tea; baking bread and apple butter. It had made Mister Barnett think of a girl he had known many long loves ago. She had had pigtails that were just the right length to dunk in a school desk inkwell—and a turned-up nose that hadn't had sense enough to come in out of a shower of freckles.

Many have wondered, throughout the ages, why the unknown manufacturer of the priceless doors of opportunity has been such a cheapskate in providing hinges. The portal may be worth a king's ransom—but it swings on a flimsy word—a simple gesture—a moment too late or too early—or a hurried nod or shake of a head.

Quite unaware that they were approaching one of three fabulous doors—or that Dysmas was its slack and imperfect pivot—Mister Barnett and Pearly had walked down Old Love Road to the point where it is crossed by Cherub Trot Lane.

173

"Mister Barnett!" a faint, distant voice had called. "Wait! Hold on, Mister Barnett!"

"Now what?" Mister Barnett had grumbled to Pearly. "It's one of the Noah boys, I bet—Shem or Japheth—with some complaint from Old Cat about jouncing up your milk with all this walking! Well, believe you me, I've taken all I'm going to take from that caterwauling delinquent! They can tell him that I said 'Go sit on a sharp picket fence!'"

"Mister Barnett! Thanks be to goodness, I've caught up with you at last!" Dysmas, holding fast to the brim of Barnett's white top hat with both hands to keep it from flying off his head, had come loping down Cherub Trot Lane. "I wanted to return what I borrowed before you accused me of being a thief."

"My hat!" Mister Barnett had exclaimed. "It's been missing since that day you took me to the Ark to get Pearly!"

"I know," Dysmas had protested, "but I've been chasing you all over the Celestial City to give it back! Anyway, it doesn't become me. The saintly Peter says I look like an Irish leprechaun hibernating under a frosted tree stump."

"Ha!" had been Mister Barnett's ungracious comment as he snatched the hat from Dysmas' hands, smoothed it on his coat sleeve and placed it at its proper angle on his white head. In this adjustment, his glance had traveled to the opposite corner of Old Love Road and Cherub Trot Lane. He had frozen into speechless immobility.

"Mister Barnett?" Dysmas had given Barnett's arm a shake. "Do you know you're starching up on me? As you know, my nerves have been on the ragged side ever since old Pilate pointed his finger at me—and if you plan to metamorphose yourself, I do think you should have warned me! I would suppose, since Lot's wife looked back and turned to salt, that you—looking forward—are changing yourself into pepper?"

"Look, Pearly!" Mister Barnett had cried. "Lift up your woe-begone head and feast your weary yak peepers! Right there in front of us—after all our trotting and tramping—is The Lot! Even the newest Johnny-come-lately would know in a split jiffy that that place was created with a big top in mind! Not a yard too narrow nor a rod too short! And if we hadn't met up with Dysmas, we might not have noticed it! Pearly—give the man a kiss to show our appreciation!"

The dutiful Pearly stuck out her wide-as-a-paintbrush tongue and slapped an ear-to-ear kiss across Dysmas' face.

"That's the ticket! Now come on, Pearly—let's you and me be the first ones to set foot on the midway of the Grandest Show in the Universe!"

Dysmas, feeling his nose to see if Pearly might have kissed it out of alignment, had watched Mister Barnett and Pearly hurry across the street—and then, in joyous abandon, throw themselves down in the tall, green grass.

"There goes a man," said Dysmas, "who has bats where his halo ought to be! Poor crazy fellow—I kind of wish he had turned himself into a pillar of pepper!"

The next morning found Mister Barnett up and about very early. His pot of plans for his circus had simmered over a glowing fire of splendid dreams the whole night long and now it was bubbling over.

He threw on his clothes, shook Pearly out of her snoring and combed the sleep-snarls out of her small bushy tail.

"Last night," he told the yak, "after you fell asleep on me, I asked our landlady where one would go if one wanted a circus tent. She told me the most likely place would be The Impossible Shop, run by Barnabas on the Street of Miracles. Now—suppose we skip our breakfast—" Pearly gave him such a reproachful look that he quickly retracted this suggestion. "Or perhaps just a small one so's we can be there when the shop opens."

He gave Pearly a package of Yellow-weed Yak Food which he had purchased from Mrs. Noah. The lady had guaranteed that it had all the vitamins and nutritional value of a cubic yard of mixed hay and alfalfa. While Pearly chomped away with gusto, Mister Barnett forced himself to eat a slightly stale bun, bought for a blessing some days before at the Bakery of the Five Loaves at Number 6, St. Mark Way.

Pearly's appetite appeased, they set forth at a jog and a yak-trot for the Street of Miracles. When they arrived, they found The Impossible Shop closed and shuttered.

"How do you like that?" exclaimed the indignant Mister Barnett. "Here it is, the middle of the dawn and he's not up yet!" He beat on the door with his fist and shouted, "Wake up! Wake up in there! Customers waiting!"

After a few minutes, the slip-slap of slippers could be heard. A drowsy key nudged a slumbering lock and the door yawned open—disclosing the saintly Barnabas in his nightshirt.

"What do you want?" he demanded. "If Gabriel sent you, you go back and tell him he can't have his horn! I gave the Proprietor my solemn promise not to let it out of my hands. He doesn't want any experimental tootling to set off a false Day of Judgment."

"I don't know anything about any horn," said Mister Barnett. "I came about a circus tent. Do you have one in stock?"

"I did have until last evening," Barnabas admitted. "Never so glad to get rid of anything in my whole career. Took up half my loft room! Great rolls of canvas—a whole forest of poles—bundles and bundles of stakes!"

"You'll have to find me another one. And without delay! My name is Barnett!"

"Oh, no!" Barnabas tried to close the door but Mister Barnett blocked it with the toe of a crocodile boot. A worried eye peered at him through the crack. "Are you the one Dysmas calls Crazy Johnny?"

"I don't know what he calls me—but I am John T. Barnett! I need a tent for my show!"

"But you've already got one! What have you done with it?"

"Pearly—" Mister Barnett turned to his yak and threw up his hands, "just listen to this potty who's called another potty crazy!" He pointed a finger at the quaking eye in the crack. "Explain that last statement about me having a tent."

"I had it taken out of my loft last evening—directly after Dysmas came by and told me that you'd finally decided on a lot at Cherub Trot Lane and Old Love Road!"

"Let me get this straight," said the perplexed Barnett. "How did you know the tent belonged to me?"

"Because, when it came to me, it had your name on it, that's why! Do you want to argue with the Proprietor's billing?"

"No!" Mister Barnett said hastily. "No, of course I don't!"

"I worked the whole night getting it carted out there!

Believe me, I never would have gone into Impossibles if I had known I might get stuck with a circus sometime! And now—when my head has scarce touched my pillow, you come beating on my door—!"

"I'm sorry!" Mister Barnett took a pad from his pocket and wrote on it. "You have my personal and abject apology." He tore the top leaf from the pad and thrust it through the crack in the door. "Here—with Pearly's and my compliments!"

"What is it?" Barnabas asked suspiciously.

"A free pass to the opening performance of the Grandest Show in the Universe!" said Mister Barnett magnanimously—as though he had just bestowed a lifetime certificate for one hour wing care and halo polishing. "It entitles you and any saintly friends you care to invite to reserved seats directly in front of the center ring! Come, Pearly—!" He took a few steps up the Street of Miracles before a sudden thought brought him to a halt. "Pearly—you're forgetting your manners," he whispered. "I think you should show your personal appreciation. While I walk ahead, why don't you run back and give that kind man a kiss?"

Mister Barnett went blithely on his way—unaware that his impulsive but rash suggestion would spark a heavenly Donnybrook—an epic hand-to-hoof struggle of man against yak. It was later to be known as The Dreadful and Disgraceful Imbroglio at Number 42.

When Barnabas saw Pearly wheel obediently and trot toward his shop with a loving smile on her face, he slammed the door, turned the lock, hooked the chain, and dropped the bar. As further insurance, he put his back against it and braced his feet. He snickered as he congratulated himself on his quick thinking and lightning muscular response.

He had forgotten that the Proprietor, when He first designed the yak, had decided that the head should have a good, strong frontal bone for offense, defense and expedience.

Pearly, moving at a medium canter, hit the door with the devastating competence of a wrecker's ball. Lock, chain, bar, and hinges ruptured with a scream of split wood and wrenched metal. Barnabas, a nightshirted arrow, was catapulted the length of the shop and came down head first into a barrel of pipettes and poppets.

Quite helpless, he might have been confined for some time in this uncomfortable and undignified position if it hadn't been for Pearly. Answering his shouts for help with loud bawls of affection and reassurance, she overturned the barrel. Then, bracing herself, she gave it a tremendous butt which sent it rolling across the shop to burst its hoops and shatter its staves on the opposite wall.

Barrel-shocked and dizzy, Barnabas crawled out of the wreckage. A lesser man, after such an ordeal, would have submitted to the inevitable and accepted osculation. Not Barnabas. He started to run—shouting lustily for the Angels of Peace.

In all the Celestial City, there is no better place for an obstacle race than The Impossible Shop on the Street of Miracles. Barnabas, fleet as a hare and Pearly, yare as a yak, raced up and down the narrow aisles between floor-to-ceiling stacks of cases, hampers, crates, trunks, boxes, chests, cabinets, casks, baskets, and bins. For awhile, Barnabas was well in the lead because in negotiating the turns, he had a smaller wheelbase.

Glancing back over his shoulder, he had noted how this advantage had improved the situation. Until the Angels of Peace got off their lazy behinds and onto their fat wings to rescue him, he had only to set a pace which would keep him ahead of the amorous beastie.

Running easily, his skulking self-confidence imprudently showed its head—and was immediately decapitated by a thundering crash and clatter. Turning his own, Barnabas saw to his horror that the race must go to the one with the longer wheelbase. As she banked on the turns, Pearly was skidding her hind quarters, toppling the piled containers of Impossibles into the aisles and slowly reducing the course to zero.

Barnabas didn't give up until he was cornered. When ten Angels of the Peace arrived, he was pinned to the floor by one of Pearly's hoofs. She was kissing him with her sandpaper tongue; tenderly, ardently, and thoroughly. Then, having done her duty dutifully and hoping to overtake Mister Barnett before he got to the Lot, she put down her head and went out the door like a bowling ball—scoring a perfect strike on the ten Angels of the Peace.

As could be expected, a report on this outrageous and scandalous episode—voluminous and complete in every base detail—was sent to the Proprietor. With it went a request that Pearly be instantly detached from Mister Barnett's custody and exiled to the last water hole in the Forest of Forever and Aye. The reply, written by the swift, sure hand of the Proprietor, said:

"Request denied. I say unto you that an expression of love by man or creature is never a sin but ever a virtue in this Celestial City."

The first performance of John T. Barnett's Grandest Show in the Universe was a gala affair. The Main Tent, as white and spotless as a cumulus cloud ironed to the thinness of a damask napkin, seemed to float over the crowd which occupied every seat.

Thousands of gleaming starlights were strung from tent pole to tent pole—and each pole was so large and so newly gilded that a cherub might think it was a lightning bolt which had lost its zigs and zags on the anvil of some daring halosmith.

These starlights illumined the sea of faces—some of which were known to every citizen in the Celestial City: Matthew, Mark, Luke, and John. Job, Joshua, Isaiah, Ezekiel, and Jude. Peter, Timothy, Simon Peter, and Daniel. Dysmas, Captain and Mrs. Noah, and Solomon and all his wives.

There was a roll of drums and a fanfare of trumpets—and then the band, in scarlet and gold coats, filled the great tent with a wing-tingling rendition of "Pearly Forever"—a circus march composed especially for the occasion by John T. Barnett himself.

The crowd leaned forward expectantly, waiting for the ringmaster's whistle. It knew it was about to witness a show which would be second to none on any celestial sphere.

No one was disappointed. Not one had ever seen high-wire artists so daring—or clowns so comical—or contortionists so flexible—or acrobats so gyrational. Everyone agreed that the animals were the smartest, the equestrians the most nimble-footed, and the daring young girl, fair as a daughter of Eve in her apple-green tights, was the last heavenly word on her flying trapeze.

Mister Barnett and Pearly stood at the front entrance when the show was over. People came up to him, shook his hand warmly, and said:

"Marvelous!"

"Extraordinary!"

"Stupendous!"

"Astonishing!"

"Indescribable!"

"Superlative!"

Even Mrs. Noah was impressed by the performance. Wearing her best summer-garden-after-a-cloudburst bonnet, she elbowed herself through the throng of admirers and gave him a chop on the shoulder.

"Pretty good show!" she cried. "If I do say so myself, Mister John T. Pearly—you got a pretty good show!"

All this should have made John T. Barnett very happy. As he and his yak wended their way homeward, he should have been dancing down the celestial streets. Instead, he shuffled and moped along as though he were too weary and too depressed to activate his crocodile boots.

Pearly knew that he must have some good reason for jumping out of the haymow of triumph to bury himself in the dungheap of desolation. When they were in their room at the boardinghouse at The Tanbark, she laid herself down in her most attentive listening position and girded up her lachrymal organs to shed large yak tears of sympathy.

"Pearly," said Mister Barnett, "Pearly, my dear, we are in trouble. Deep trouble. We got us a real good circus. An excellent circus. Watching it tonight, I would say without any

fear of my conscience contradicting myself, that it is right up
to par with the one that was known from coast to coast and
around the globe— 'John T. Barnett's Greatest Show on
Earth.'"

Pearly made a catcher's mitt of her tongue and caught the
two sad drops of water which fell from her green and her
blue eyes.

"But—and this is the fix we're in, Pearly—we didn't
promise folks the Greatest Show on Earth. We told this whole
Celestial City that we were going to present The Grandest
Show in the Universe."

Pearly moaned in D minor—her sides going in and out
like a grief stricken accordion.

"I know!" Mister Barnett patted her. "It's hard to face but
we just got to do it! For the first time in our lives, we're fooling our public! We're not delivering what we advertise!"

This was more than Pearly could take while lying down.
She rose blindly to her feet and staggered to the window.
Pushing aside the curtains, she let her copious tears cascade
to the ground below. Their landlady, awakened by the
downpour, jumped out of her bed and closed her casement
against what she thought was a summer shower.

"Now, Pearly—," Mister Barnett hastened to embrace her,
"there's no reason for you to take the whole blame on your
horns! We're partners, aren't we? We'll work it out! All we
got to do is find something really unique! Something
absolutely unbelievable! Something that never before has
been seen by anybody in any circus! Now—that isn't such a
large order for us, is it?" He took the window curtain and
held it against her moist nose. "Now stop your crying and

blow real hard."

Pearly blew—and their landlady, down below, thinking a wind had come up, again jumped out of her bed and closed her casement shutters.

"There, now," crooned Mister Barnett. "You stretch out and close your big baby blue and green eyes. Tomorrow's another day—and we'll start out bright and neat and find us an all-star, unequaled, unparalleled attraction and— presto-chango—we got us our Grandest Show!"

Something unique.

Something absolutely unbelievable.

Something never before seen by anyone at any circus.

It was a large order. A very large order.

Mister Barnett and Pearly covered every part of the vast Celestial City.

They walked every footpath of the Elysian Fields. They followed every trail of the great Forest of Forever and Aye. They searched every street, avenue, roadway, millennium circle, lane, and way. They explored, scoured, rummaged, hunted, grilled, badgered, ransacked, pursued, and left no head nor halo unturned.

As the days went by, Mister Barnett's jovial face turned from blush pink to yellow-dog yellow. His extravagant mustache had a raindrop droop. His crocodile boots developed a nerve-scratching squeak which seemed to singsong "You won't find it! You won't find it! You won't find it!..."

Pearly grew thin and her cheeks grew hollow—making it appear as though she were constantly sucking soda through a straw. Her horns had the translucence of yak anemia.

Each day, when Mister Barnett took her to the old Ark to be milked, Mrs. Noah's grim face grew more grim as she saw Pearly's production of rich saffron yak cream go into an eclipse. At last, there was only a trickle...

then a dribble...

then a drip...

then a drop...

and then... merely a slight dew.

Old Cat was furious. The whole thing was a dastardly plot to upset the routine of his heavenly days. He became so hot under his star-studded collar which had been a Valentine present from his mistress that the leather smoldered and smoked.

He walked up and down the Street of Miracles in front of Captain Noah's Ark—caterwauling his wrathful indignation—and proclaiming to the whole Celestial City that the Philistines had come down on his fold and embezzled his yak cream!

That night, when he had curled into the concavity of Miss Barnworth's stomach as they lay on their bed in Canaan Common, he attacked the problem with feline intensity. It was obvious that today's shenanigans weren't going to restore things to normalcy. The Philistines didn't give a kitten-mew about his yak cream. So—to Gehenna with the Philistines!

His ears perked—and he seemed to hear again the advice his mother had purred to him long, long ago as he had nursed contentedly. "The Proprietor helps cats who help themselves. If you wish a meat scrap, you must find an alley with a garbage can behind a butcher shop. If a fishhead is your desire, you must search for an alley that has a fish store."

185

Ah, yes. She was a wise old tabby. She must be here in the Celestial City. The saintly Francis would have seen to that. Probably out in the Forest of Forever and Aye. She might not remember him after all the years and all her other kittens. When he was again rich in yak cream, he'd go out and find her. He'd bring her right here to Miss Barnworth's house. She'd often said that living with a cat made her happy—so living with two cats ought to make her delirious.

Would his mother's earthly advice work here in the Celestial City? If a cat wanted a wrong made right, where would a cat go? The Angels of the Peace? The Patriarch Prophets? No—speaking alley-wise, a cat would find any justice in their garbage cans pretty dry and unsatisfying.

Then who?

Again Old Cat's ears perked—and again he seemed to hear a wise old purr.

"The Proprietor helps cats who help themselves."

Why, of course.

Simple as all that.

When you want something, you go right to the top.

With a satisfied sigh, Old Cat shut off his thinking motor. He pushed with his feet until he and Miss Barnworth's stomach were one. Then, his problem solved for the nonce, he closed his yellow blinkers and slept.

On the morning of the next day, the brawny Shard of Number One Chariot was one of the many who waited in the anteroom of the cloudtop tower to ask some favor of the Proprietor.

He, himself, had come to seek permission to fill the great

thundering vehicle with sweet grasses from the Pastures of Eden and to take all the cherubs of Angels' Aide on a moonlight chariot ride.

Shard watched Old Cat swagger across the Plaza of Eternity—pause momentarily to give his whiskers a lick and a promissory lap—and then, with the utmost arrogance, as though he and not the Proprietor had labored on their creation, ascended the spiral stairs which led upward and upward to the cloudtop tower. Arriving at the anteroom, Old Cat set his sights on the door of the Proprietor's workroom— and assuming a pugilistic roll, sauntered through the waiting crowd with bunched muscles on the alert to spar with any leg that got in his way.

"You'll have to wait your turn!" Shard hissed.

Old Cat returned the hiss with interest and continued on his way. He found the Proprietor's door slightly ajar. He pushed it with his paw until the opening was equal to the width of his whiskers and slithered into the room. The Proprietor was seated at His desk—and standing in front of it was Mister Partridge, who had a flea circus off Second Millennium Circle.

Ever since he got out of bed—in fact, from the very instant that Miss Barnworth awakened him by shoving him out of the warm hollow of her beloved stomach—Old Cat had been worried. It was all very well to be told by a purr in the night to talk to the Proprietor—but did the Proprietor speak cat?

It was quite likely, in all His horsing around in old Shard's chariot, that He'd picked up all the different kinds of gibberish spoken by two-legged creatures. It was highly improbable,

187

however, that He'd wasted His moonlit nights sitting on some backyard fence listening to a tomcat gab fest.

Anyway, omniscience might be only an empty knothole which had been blown up into a beautiful mouse hole in someone's catnip dream. He leaped to the top of a tall chest and settled himself to watch and listen.

"Yes, Mister Partridge?" said the Proprietor.

"I didn't come about myself, Sir," explained the flea circus man. "It's my star performer." He took a small box from his pocket—and with careful fingers and tweezer, removed a black dot. "She's the smartest flea in my whole troupe. She's got bad trouble."

"Oh?" The Proprietor smiled. "Let her tell Me about it."

Old Cat rose and stretched himself, preparing to leave. As he had thought, he was wasting his time on a basket-time tale for kittens—wherein the Big Cat in the sky reached into a golden trash barrel and pulled out miracles. He stopped in mid-stretch as he heard the Proprietor say:

"Now, don't be frightened, Becky. If you want Me to solve your problem, you must look at Me—and think, very clearly and with absolute trust, what you wish Me to know... Your name isn't Becky?... Oh—your name was Becky but for professional reasons you're changed it to Columbine... Well, then, Becky-now-Columbine, what is your trouble?...Your right hind leg is much the stronger of the two...and in your act, when you leap, you constantly slice to the left...That must be most embarrassing—and it shall be remedied immediately. It is My wish, Becky-now-Columbine, that from this instant on, your left leg power shall be equal to the right. Throughout eternity, your leaps will be the straightest and most breathtaking in the flea circus. So be it."

The instant the door closed behind Mister Partridge and his minute leaping lady, Old Cat jumped from the top of the chest and made a perfect four foot landing at the exact center of the Proprietor's desk. Fixing unwinking yellow eyes on the face of the Proprietor, he revved up his thought motor to its fullest broadcast capacity:

"My name is Old Cat. I am good, kind, gentle, and trustworthy. If my coat appears slightly dusty, it is because I shivered the whole night through on a poor bed of sackcloth and ashes. Although I have never lifted a paw or claw in anger, I prayed that I would become even more meek and mild—because I embrace the saintly belief that no cat is a whole alley unto himself. When people have tramped on my tail, I have endured the pain as a true martyr and have humbly purred their pardon for being in the path of their big fat feet. The only Commandment I'm shaky on is Number Five—but I intend on honoring my mother as soon as I can locate her. If You have any knowledge of the identity of my father, I will be more than willing to honor him, too. Now—no doubt You would be interested to hear a day-to-day account of my life to the present moment. I was born on the second day of December. That makes me a Sagittarius. I had two brothers and three sisters—so that made the whole litter Sagittarians. That's the Archer. Of course, we weren't archers, we were kittens. I have been told that I was the most handsome and promising..."

Old Cat got what he wanted. Some said it was because the Proprietor thought Old Cat was the most amusing

189

visitor He had had in His cloudtop tower in a full decade of heavenly days.

Shard didn't agree. He said the old yellow-eyed fraud would have gone on thought-talking for all eternity if the Proprietor hadn't thrown him a miracle just to get shut of him.

It has been noted, however, that whenever the Proprietor looks down from His cloudtop tower and sees Old Cat padding pugnaciously across the great Plaza of Eternity, He always smiles—which is a very good thing for lambs, cats, and humans who sometimes stray from the fold.

Today, when newcomers arrive in the Celestial City, one of the first things they wish to see is the palatial Victorian mansion which belongs to John T. Barnett and Pearly at Canaan Common. The young ones swing on the gate which is a red and gold wheel from a circus wagon—and drink from the fountain which spouts pink lemonade. Every hour on the hour, there is much shouting and scrambling. Mister Barnett has trained a flock of doves to fly overhead and to drop free tickets to the circus.

At every performance, the Big Top at Old Love Road and Cherub Trot Lane is so filled that it almost bursts its side walls. Not one person in the whole enormous crowd has ever seen high-wire artists so daring—or clowns so comical—or contortionists so flexible—and the daring young girl, fairest daughter of Eve in her apple-green tights, is the very last heavenly word on her flying trapeze.

Everyone waits for the Grand Finale—for it is this Closing Spectacle which makes the John T. Barnett Circus not just the Greatest Show on Earth—but the Grandest Show in the Universe!

The Big Top slowly dims its many lights and it becomes as dark as the vast interior of Jonah's whale. There is no sound save the breathing of the waiting crowd. Then, a single star-spot points a white finger at the center ring. Mister Barnett stands there with his white top hat in his hand. The golden chain across his cookhouse-catsup vest is strained to the breaking point as he fills his lungs and says:

"Ladies and Gentlemen! The Barnett Circus is proud to present the most stupendous, extraordinary, incredible, awe-inspiring attraction in the history of the circus! You will be amazed, dumbfounded, electrified, staggered, and stunned by what you are about to see! I direct your attention to the far entrance as the Grandest Show in the Universe brings you its unparalleled Grand Finale!"

A thousand star-spots spring to instant light and race each other to that far entrance!

Then, stepping light-foot into the immense arena, comes Pearly. Her dainty hoofs gleam, her coat is combed, her tail brushed, and on her shining horns are tinkling silver bells.

Following close on her heels is a fat, full-sized Mastodon.

Hanging onto the Mastodon's tail, is a well-fed, mild-mannered Brontosaurus.

Ambling along behind the Brontosaurus, is a docile Pterodactyl in a yellow sweater knitted for him by Mrs. Noah because she though the skinny creature looked naked and shivery.

And gamboling along after the Pterodactyl, come a Gigantosaurus, a Tyrannosaurus and a Triceratops—appearing slap-happy with delight to come from extinction to distinction at the Grandest Show in the Universe.

John T. Barnett hosts the Grandest Show in the Universe.

John T. Barnett, owning such a show, is very happy.

Pearly, because she loves Mister Barnett, is ecstatically happy.

Old Cat, because Pearly's bliss means plenty of yak cream, is gleefully happy.

Miss Barnworth, Old Cat's mistress, is also happy—although she has developed leg cramps.

As Old Cat had thought, he found his dear mother in the Forest of Forever and Aye.

He still sleeps against Miss Barnworth's stomach—and dearest mother curls up in the hollow behind her knees.

In her sleep she purrs a lullaby—and in it she says that Old Cat is the sweetest, smartest kitten there ever was or ever will be.

Miss Barnworth sometimes covers her head with her pillow but she never moves her legs an inch.

As the Proprietor has often said—an expression of love—or a lullaby of love—is a very precious thing anywhere.

And most especially in His Celestial City.

VI

Dusk is a soft and gentle time in the majestic Celestial City. It is pleasant to sit in the renowned Plaza of Eternity as Joktan, the lamplighter, with his small ladder under his arm, whistles a pre-creation melody as he goes about his nightly task of lighting the starlamps along the winding paths.

Lud, Angel of the Peace for the Plaza at this eventide hour, nods and smiles at friends and acquaintances who have come early from distant Kingdom Come or Safe Corral to be sure of occupying their favorite bench. Lud's job is a sinecure. Not once, within the memory of the Celestial City's oldest inhabitant, has the peace of the peaceful Plaza ever been disturbed.

Now and then he stops to wag an admonishing finger at a

boy-cherub who has shinnied up a starlamp—or to fish a small girl-cherub from a lily-filled basin of one of the Plaza's many fountains.

The towering, mighty Wall of Heaven is now black against the purple sky—and the vines, planted by the Proprietor Himself when this supreme metropolis was naught but a tiny village, unfold their flowers. The evening breeze, after stopping to fill his censer with their perfume, dances down every path like a giddy bishop dispensing incense.

To no two noses—out of all the thousands of noses in the Plaza this nightfall—does it smell the same. Otto Schnitter, the school bus driver, says it's apple blossoms. Captain Noah maintains it's cinnamon flowers. Sukie, cherub of Angels' Aide, insists it's exactly like the lily of the valley sachet in her mother's dresser drawer. Cap'n Cabe of the Magnolia Blossom Showboat swears that it has the heady aroma of greasepaint and powder. Peter, guardian at the great Gates, believes it is a blend of frankincense and myrrh. To Angela Barnworth, secretary, it smells like the gardenia in her very first corsage for her high school prom—and to her friend-companion, Old Cat, it is the delightful and enchanting aroma of catnip.

As noses sniff and their owners are transported momentarily to some former time and place, that stalwart trio, Shadrach, Meshach, and Abednego, may saunter by. Behind them and imitating in miniature their swagger and every gesture, troops a tidy clutch of cherubs. Each hero-worshipping heart cherishes the fond hope that the great ram's horn will sound its hoarse bleat any second from a distant watchtower. This would mean that some remote minor sun was blazing out of control. It is one of the thrills of a cherub's heavenly lifetime to watch Shadrach, Meshach, and Abednego roar out the Gates in their monstrous fire-chariots of gleaming scarlet and polished brass.

An opinion poll, taken on any corner and in any part of the vast Celestial City, would show that most residents believe that this trio of intrepid dousers is unequaled. And they are right. Having easily survived the fiery furnace of the infamous King Nebuchadnezzar in Daniel's time, a hot, flaming sun is no more than a flash fire in a tin wastebasket to dauntless Shadrach, Meshach, and Abednego.

They, in turn, if a poll were taken on miracles, would say that such things come in all sizes and shapes and colors. A miracle can be as big and as plump as a hippopotamus—or as small and as bright as a ladybug.

To prove this, they point to the lady who has just emerged from the Street of Miracles, crossed Eden Way, and is now entering the Plaza. Her name is Mrs. Noah—and she, her husband, and her three sons, Shem, Ham, and Japheth, have charge of the Ark, that remarkable and celebrated pet shelter at Number 10.

Mrs. Noah is a fine figure of a woman with a forcible manner, a brisk, no-nonsense air and an eye which can strip all the glitter from sham and sentiment. In the Celestial City, it is no secret that she has her husband and her three sons under her solid and able thumb.

As this lady comes nearer, walking a slow and measured way along the bench-lined path, it can be seen that she is accompanied by a large German shepherd dog. The dog is a female and her name is Susannah.

This Susannah wears a harness which is easily recognizable

as the kind which is worn by a seeing-eye dog. Mrs. Noah has a firm hold on the strap—and she allows Susannah to guide her through the crowded Plaza. The lady looks neither to right nor left—but as she passes, her straight and defiant back dares anyone to find anything strange or bizarre in her behavior.

But it is strange and bizarre—and people who are not avid devotees of the Plaza are more than a little surprised. They will be even more surprised one hour from now. Susannah will lead an embarrassed Mr. Noah along this same route. Following that, at sixty minute intervals, she will lead the hulking but cowed Shem, the robust but awed Ham, and the strapping but intimidated Japheth along this same winding path.

"Why?" some newcomer will ask, when he is quite certain no member of the stony-faced and chip-on-the-shoulder Noah family is about. "Why do they do that?"

Well, it's a reasonable question and deserves a reasonable answer. Susannah has always been a seeing-eye dog. She has been here a very short time. She is a very intelligent dog—but a deeply planted sense of duty and years of absolute devotion make it impossible for her to believe that there is no such thing as blindness in the Celestial City.

She belonged, in her earthly time, to David Blake. He operated a magazine and tobacco stand in the lobby of a post office, situated in a town not far from San Francisco. Susannah was barely out of puppy-mash and into T-bones when their association began. Even at that age, she was a serious dog with a great deal of dignity. A born lady was the way David put it.

They lived in a furnished room ten blocks from the post

office. It wasn't much but to Susannah—who, like all dogs, has no sense of values, it was a small paradise. The wallpaper was faded, the carpet threadbare, and the curtains cheap and sleazy. David Blake, being blind, couldn't see these things and was quite happy. His feet and hands knew every inch of this little black box called "home"—and outside, to move about in the big black box, there was Susannah to safely lead the way.

Every morning, before the walk to the post office, David released her for a ten minute run in the small park which was across the street from the rooming house. He waited while her nose read and digested all the news of events that had transpired during the night—and then he would whistle "O Susannah, don't you cry for me—" By the time he had a banjo on an Alabamy knee, her cold nose was on his hand.

She had two more periods of freedom. One, when they came home in the evening—and the other, after the eleven P.M. news on the radio. The day over, Susannah stretched herself out by the side of David's bed. Very close to the bed so that a hand needed to fall no distance at all to touch her rough coat and know that a friend was on watch through the lonely hours.

Sundays, when the weather was fine, was a wonderful day. There was another and larger park some distance away. Susannah enjoyed the grave responsibility placed upon her by the trip back and forth by bus. She must be certain that David was waiting on the curb at the exact spot the bus would stop and the door would open. She must be sure that he was safely in a seat before the bus gave its forward lurch. She must take him off the bus without the slightest mishap. If he were to stumble, her whole wonderful day would be spoiled.

In the park, they walked until David was tired—and then they sat on a bench and listened to all the Sunday sounds of children and people. Susannah watched less fortunate dogs running after rubber balls, chasing squirrels, and dashing at pigeons to frighten them—and she thought how lucky she was to have an important job and not to have to spend her life having fun.

One evening, bringing David home from the post office, the ten blocks seemed to have lengthened to ten miles. Her legs, always so sure and strong, strained to take her up the stairs. The siren song of the can opener on a dog food can fell on deaf ears and she ate no supper. The after-eleven-o'clock airing, instead of being a happy time, was an ordeal which seemed to sap all her strength.

David awoke in the night and, as he always did, reached down to touch her. A hot nose and a dry, rough tongue told him she was awake and on watch. He rested a hand on her shoulder and he could feel a deep trembling. Taking a blanket from his bed, he covered her.

He wondered what could be wrong with Susannah. They'd been together a long time—but she wasn't old. Not really old. Without sight, he couldn't see how the white hairs had grayed the brown muzzle—or how a film was slowly covering the sharp, bright eyes.

He reached out once more and let his fingers explore the blanket. The trembling had stopped. That was good. Perhaps, after a night's sleep, she'd be herself again. He wouldn't open the stand tomorrow—he'd stay home and let her rest and take care of her.

After awhile, he dozed off into a restless, troubled sleep.

Not until morning did he know that Susannah would never again go to the post office or the park in David's world—and no matter how loudly and how pleadingly he whistled "Oh Susannah," she would never again lead him along the streets of that town near San Francisco.

Francis, of course, knew this was going to happen. That evening, while he had been waiting for his great, swift heavenly carrier to be prepared for its journey down to earth to fetch every loved pet to the wonderful Ark on the Street of Miracles, he had been going over the day's list with the good senior-saint, Peter.

"Oh, no!" Francis had cried when he came to Susannah's name. "Not this one, Peter! Not now!"

"Don't you look at me!" Peter had shaken a finger at him in protest. "You know very well that I don't make out the travel papers!"

"Susannah's needed where she is!" Francis had stated flatly. "I tell you she's indispensable!"

"No one, excepting the Proprietor, is that," had been Peter's testy reply. "The dog is old and tired."

"She's been doing her job!" Francis had argued. "No younger dog could do better!"

"The Proprietor believes she deserves rest and a little fun!"

"Susannah doesn't know how to rest—she's a working dog! And she never played a game in her whole life—her idea of fun is to take care of David Blake!"

"My dear Francis, the dog's name is on the list and there is nothing that you or I can do about it. Now, please—get aboard your carrier and take it on its way before you disrupt the whole transportation system! Take my word for it, this

Susannah will be very happy here. Very happy, indeed!"

"*Happy?*" Francis had cried scornfully as he turned on his heel and marched off toward his gleaming conveyance. "Happy, he says!" Then, over a stiff, indignant shoulder, he had called to that benevolent senior-saint, Peter, "If there's one thing that really puts a tarnish on my halo, it's that fuzzy-whiskered, perpetual optimist!"

As Francis had expected, he found David Blake wrapped in misery.

"Mr. Blake?" he said. "I know that you are unable to hear me—but do listen and perhaps you can feel what I'm saying. When you give your heart to a dog, you must expect it to be quite frayed and torn when you get it back. But, I beg you, don't worry about Susannah. Mr. and Mrs. Noah are most kind—and they'll care for your friend with a love that will be as great as yours.

"On a future day—one which only the Proprietor knows—you will be coming to the Celestial City and you will be wanting to reclaim Susannah. The old Ark is very easy to find. Through the Plaza and then across Eden Way. Number 10 is but a few steps down the winding Street of Miracles. There, among all the millions of other loved pets, you will find Susannah anxiously awaiting your arrival.

"But—on second thought, Mr. Blake—I do believe I can make arrangements to meet you at the top of the Stairs. Yes—that would be best, because I know of a short-cut through the Plaza which will save a whole two minutes. Isn't that heartening? Just like that, we've sliced a full one hundred and twenty lonely seconds from the period you and Susannah will be separated!

"I'll be standing along-side a fuzzy-whiskered old codger, who will have a silly, optimistic grin on his face and a large bunch of souvenir keys for the nonexistent lock on our great Gates jangling in his simple hand.

"I will be the skinny, gangling, quite unhandsome fellow with, if I haven't had the time to comb it, a few stray canary, parakeet or gosling feathers in my hair—and Peter Fuzzy-Whiskers will be looking at me out of the corner of his eye and will be whispering censorious remarks about the state of my garments.

"I could be just as spotless and beau-angelic as he if I had nothing better to do than stand at the Gates. But when a fellow has to rescue and cherish dogs, rabbits, cats, ponies, hamsters, monkeys, mice, raccoons, pigs, cows, skunks, squirrels, and every other animal that the Proprietor has made and mankind has given love to—I tell you, you're bound to pick up a few stray hairs!

"Well—I must leave you now, Mr. Blake. I have still the whole wide world to cover tonight—and many thousands of small, stilled hearts are waiting for me to carry them to the Ark, the Elysian Fields, or the Forest of Forever and Aye, where they will beat again. Good-bye, David Blake—and when you come, look for me at the top of the Stairs and together we will hasten to the Street of Miracles!"

Susannah's deep sleep continued until the carrier was in sight of the vast barrier of morning mist, which lies on the rim of the universe to make the boundary between what was and what will be. As she had slept, all the scars of her years had been healed. Her old, rough coat had become smooth and lustrous and the white hairs on her muzzle had vanished. Her legs had become strong and straight as the ache in the muscles and the scream in the joints had disappeared.

The carrier tunneled into the thick, dark mist and it was twilight in the monstrous conveyance. It was then that Susannah opened her eyes and learned that the film no longer beclouded her vision. It was a surprise and a delight to discover she could look the to-home-from-the-post-office length of the mighty vehicle and could clearly see a minute, coal-black mouse wiggling its microscopic pink nose between the bars of its half-pint cage.

People, coming to the Celestial City, look to find the Proprietor, but Susannah, as is the usual way with dogs, looked to find David Blake, who had been the beloved, all-powerful and all-knowing proprietor of her canine earthly world. He was nowhere in sight—and Susannah paced the great carrier, trying to find some lingering trace of his footsteps.

Her nose discovered no familiar smell and a terrible feeling of loss and desolation descended upon her. She came to Francis and laid her head on his knee and whimpered.

"There, there, Susannah," Francis patted her head. "Everything's going to be all right."

The carrier had just burst through the bank of morning mist and below were the Stairs, the Gates, and the eternal and beautiful City. Although he had been reprimanded many times for careless landings by Phut, Schedular Chief of Arrivals and Departures—and even though he knew Peter must be watching to criticize, Francis controlled his carrier with one hand and kept the other on Susannah's head.

"Everything's going to be fine—you just wait and see!" He then committed another unpardonable error. He took his eyes off the landing area and lifted them to the high, cloudtop tower where the Proprietor sometimes sits to learn what is happening to what He has created.

"Honored Sir," said Francis. "As You know, I don't ask many favors. If You chanced to hear what I just told this dog—please—I beg You—don't let me be a liar!"

The Proprietor may have heard and may have answered in His own inimitable way. Phut and Peter both congratulated Francis for the first perfect landing that he had ever made during his heavenly career.

204

At the ancient, paint bare old Ark on the Street of Miracles, Susannah was received by the Noahs with the capable kindness that was showered on every new boarder.

"Handsome animal." Mrs. Noah scratched Susannah's neck. "What'd you say was her name, Francis?"

"Susannah."

"Oh," said the lady. "Named after the good wife of Joachim, book of Dan'l, I suppose?"

"Yes," smiled Mr. Noah. "The one who was surprised in her bath by the elders!"

"Trust you to remember that!" snorted his helpmate.

"No," Francis said hastily. "The dog wasn't named after that Susannah. She was named for the one in an old song. It was very popular down on earth when folks were going west in their covered wagons. When they came up here, they brought it with them. Sometimes, at night, I walk out to Trail's End. All those covered wagons are a real pretty sight in the moonlight—and somewhere, a banjo plucking away— 'O Susannah, don't you cry for me—'"

"I don't care for that earthbilly music." Mrs. Noah tossed her head. "Lot of nonsense. Give me a good, inspirational hymn. Now, back to this dog—you said she's a city animal?"

"That's right."

"Then I'll quarter her on the street side where she can watch people go by. Ought to make her feel more at home, don't you think?"

"That is a brilliant idea, Mrs. Noah. And if, once in awhile, you could pet her and talk to her—?"

"Well, I can't promise that. Oh—I'll say 'hello' maybe, as I go by. I'm a busy woman. I've got 10,286 other dogs, 11,010 cats, 7,642 parakeets, 9,538 canaries..."

Two days later, when Francis appeared with that day's consignment of fur and feathers, Mrs. Noah took his arm and drew him aside.

"Francis," said the lady, "I'm worried about that dog."

"Which dog?"

"That Susannah."

"What's she been doing?"

"That's just it—she doesn't do anything! When I pet her and talk to her—and I must have done it fifty times today—she acts like she doesn't even hear me. She doesn't eat. She doesn't drink."

"That's bad." Francis bit his lip. "Very bad."

"Thank you," snapped Mrs. Noah. "Your words are a great comfort to me. Now, I've been giving the matter a lot of thought—and I think I might have the answer. What kind of utensils did she have to eat and drink out of where she came from?"

"A drinking bowl and an eating dish."

"Metal or china?"

"Metal, I believe. Yes—I'm sure of it—metal."

"Well—that's the answer then!" said Mrs. Noah triumphantly. "I've been letting her have my company china that I hardly ever use because Mr. Noah and my boys are so clumsy they might break it! I'll go right out and get Susannah a metal bowl and dish!"

Mrs. Noah put on her summer-garden-after-a-cloudburst hat, which many people swore was a bit of flotsam she had salvaged from the Flood—and bustled down the Street of Miracles to Eden Way.

At the broad Avenue of Mercy, she turned left—and after passing the First and Second Millennium Circles, she arrived at Halosmith Road.

Mrs. Noah slackened her pace and examined the signboards over the shops on this historic and famous street. There were scores of smithies—each boasting that it had the exclusive appointment to some distinguished personage in the Celestial City—but none seemed to appeal to her fancy until she came to one which was well known to the haut monde as "Japheth's."

Unlike the other smiths, Mr. Japheth did not deign to clutter his show window with a great profusion of his wares. On display was one single halo upon a background of cerise velvet. A small card, for the benefit of such customers who might not be fully aware of the shop's high character and prices, announced "Fittings by appointment only."

Mrs. Noah settled her summer-garden-after-a-cloudburst hat more firmly on her head and marched into Japheth's. The bell, over the door, tinkled a discreet notification—and then crashed to the floor with a loud clang-bang as she slammed the door behind her. Mrs. Noah eyed it malevolently and kicked it under a showcase.

A startled Japheth, wearing a cerise smock with golden halo buttons, appeared like a jack-in-the-box from his workshop in the rear of his establishment.

"Yes, Madam—" he said breathlessly. "May I be of service?"

"You might," answered Mrs. Noah, "only I'm not used to being waited upon by a man who gets up so late he's still wearing his red bed gown."

"This—" snapped Japheth, "is not a bed gown—it's a smock and I designed it myself!"

"Such being true," responded the lady, "I hope you're a better halosmith than you are a seamstress."

"Madam—!"

"Mrs. Noah. The Ark. Street of Miracles."

"Mrs. Noah, then! May I ask what you desire?"

"I desire a bowl and a dish for a dog."

"Oh, now, really, my good woman! You must be joking! I am Japheth, the—and I repeat, *the* halosmith!"

"If you can make a halo, you can make a pan and a dish," Mrs. Noah said calmly. "Goodness knows, I could do it myself if I had the material and the tools. It's very simple. You take two halos and put bottoms on them. A deep bottom for the bowl and a shallow bottom for the dish."

"This is ridiculous!" cried Japheth. "You dare to come here—knowing my reputation—"

"If I were you, I wouldn't bring up my reputation," interrupted Mrs. Noah. "I knew you when you were nothing but a wandering tinker with a mangy camel down Shinar-way.

And a very bad tinker, too! I've still got that kettle you fixed for me back in the old days on earth—and it still leaks!"

"Madam—" said the outraged Japheth, "to go back thousands of years and berate a man for a trifling failure in his youth—!"

"Are you going to oblige me," asked the imperturbable Mrs. Noah, "or do I have to go home and get that kettle? I'll sit on your doorstep and hold it in my lap—and when folks ask me what I'm doing—"

"All right! *All right*!" Japheth threw up his hands. "I'll make the bowl and the dish!" He shuddered. "Oh, the shame of it! The peerless Japheth—by appointment to a dog!"

"Never mind about that," said the lady placidly. "Just see that you do a better job on them than you did on my kettle!"

The two utensils, turned out by the halosmith, were truly beautiful and would be classed as works of art by any competent judge. In fact, Japheth was so exceedingly proud of his creations that he complacently imprinted his name on the bottoms of both the bowl and the dish. He was so overflowing with self-conceit that he called these signatures to Mrs. Noah's attention—nonchalantly flicking away imaginary flecks of dust with a cerise handkerchief.

"You observe these, Madam?" he asked, loftily. "They double the market value of these priceless *objets d'art*! Take my word for it—in years to come, they will command a saint's weight in blessings as heirlooms!"

"I doubt that they last that long without springing a leak," said the redoubtable Mrs. Noah—and with the bowl under one arm and dish under the other, she clumped out the door and back to the Ark on the Street of Miracles.

208

The new metal utensils, to Mrs. Noah's disappointment and chagrin, failed to arouse Susannah's interest. She lapped a few measly drops of water and merely sniffed at the food in the golden dish. Then, with a long sigh that was a heartbroken requiem, she laid herself down and closed her sorrowful eyes.

"We've got to cheer her up," said Mrs. Noah. "Maybe if we got her to play a game—"

"She doesn't know how to play games." Mr. Noah was examining Susannah's history in his register. "It says right here that she's never played a game in her whole life."

"She can learn. Shem—," she turned to her eldest son, "hand me that ball."

"Yes'm."

"Now—I'm going to throw it. You get down on all fours like a dog and run after it."

"Maw!" protested Shem. "I can't run like a dog!"

"You can if you put your mind to it and pull in your stomach! Now—here goes the ball and you chase after it as fast as you can!"

Wheezing and grunting, the portly Shem went galumphing across the room, resembling a baby brontosaurus with the rickets.

"Do it more graceful and frolicky!" ordered his mother. "And smile big so the dog can see how much fun you're having. Now—pick up the ball, Shem. No—for goodness sakes—not with your hand! Grab it with your teeth, you ninny! How do you expect me to teach the dog anything if you don't do it right? All right—now trot back as though you're real proud of yourself and drop the ball in my hand!"

Mrs. Noah tries to determine the source of
Susannah's despair.

"It's not going to work, Mother." Mr. Noah wagged his head. "The dog didn't even watch."

"That's Shem's fault. In my whole life, I've never seen a worse imitation of a dog!" She looked down on her eldest son, who was lying prostrate at her feet. "You can get up now—the game's over." Shem's answer was a moan. "You hear me? I said you can get up!"

"I can't, Maw," said Shem through his teeth. "I sprained something in my back."

"I should think you'd be ashamed to admit it," Mrs. Noah said bitterly. "Dogs go around that way all the time—and they don't sprain their backs! Ham—help your brother to get up—and then take him upstairs and rub him good with that horse liniment I got from Shard, the Proprietor's chariot driver."

"It says here—" Mr. Noah was still reading his registration book, "that when Susannah's owner wanted to summon her, he used to whistle the song, 'O Susannah.'"

"Now, that's something to know." Mrs. Noah's brow wrinkled in thought. "Music might be just what we want. I've heard that it can soothe a savage beast—and on a tame one, it might work just the opposite and perk 'em up! How does that song go?"

"I haven't the faintest idea."

"Don't you remember what Francis told us?" cried her youngest son. "He said that they sing it every night around the campfires out at Trail's End!"

"So he did—that was real smart of you to remember. You and I will go out there right now!"

"But, Maw—!"

"Don't but me any buts. You're the musical one of the family. You had those five lessons on the shepherd's pipe from Mr. Iscah. If the Proprietor hadn't decided right then to have the Flood, you might have become a fine artist. When it poured down for forty days and forty nights, I just knew in my bones that your musical education had gone with the tempest."

So Mrs. Noah and her youngest went out to Trail's End, where covered wagons made white circles around each ruby campfire. From booted men and their calico ladies, they learned the song that had traveled with them across the dusty plains and, carefully wrapped in fond remembrance, had been brought to the Celestial City without a cracked note or chipped word.

On the return trip, Mrs. Noah and her youngest were quite jubilant and they took turns singing "O Susannah." However, just three blocks from the Ark, they chanced to pass the Church of the Trinity as the hundred-voiced choir began their powerful rendition of "David Chased the Amalekites."

Not only the Amalekites fled. "O Susannah" ran right out of the Noahs' heads—and they again had to plod out to Trail's End to recover the melody. This time, for the return trip, they begged some cotton batting from some calico ladies, who were busily quilting by the yellow-white light from a star lantern.

With their ears stuffed with cotton, Mrs. Noah and her youngest again made their way toward the old Ark—and the lady had done such a good job of packing and tamping that the busy, crowded streets seemed as silent as outer space.

They were so stone deaf that they failed to hear the brazen alarm bells as they crossed Fourth Millennium Circle. Only by the super-angelic agility of an Angel of the Peace were they saved from being pancaked by the roaring fire-chariots of Shadrach, Meshach, and Abednego.

Indeed, it was such a narrow escape that a spark from Meshach's vehicle came tumbling down and started a brushfire in Mrs. Noah's summer-garden-after-a-cloudburst hat. Abednego, fearing that he and his friends might be singed in the fiery furnace of Mrs. Noah's temper, screeched to a stop and doused the conflagration with a quick blast from his water hose.

The outraged lady seemed to grow into a black mountain of wrath. Feet planted wide apart and arms akimbo, she opened her mouth—but no words came out because she was afraid she might again forget the Susannah song.

But Mrs. Noah was a resourceful woman. As Abednego drove off, he was more than a little amazed to hear her sing after him, in a vociferous and enraged voice—

"O, you nitwit!
You and all your clan!
O come you back this instant
And I'll fight you like a man!"

Tired, bedraggled, but triumphant, Mrs. Noah and her youngest tiptoed through the old and odorous old Ark. Praying that the hinges wouldn't squeal, they inched open the door of the room where Susannah slept. She then gave her son a good dig in the ribs with her elbow as a signal for him to begin. Her son obediently puckered his lips and whistled "O

Susannah" in a manner that was fairly allegro and passably bravura since he was performing with an elbow-bent rib.

The music had a marvelous and instantaneous effect on Susannah. Her ears jumped to alert. Her eyes popped wide open. She leaped to her feet and her tail started to wag so fast and so frantically that it was just a blur to watching eyes.

"We've done it! We've finally done it!" laughed Mrs. Noah, seizing her son and giving him a bear hug which squashed his other ribs into alignment with the bent one. "Just think—that little song was all we needed to bring her 'round! I tell you— I haven't been so happy since I was that day when I was ready to bust wide open—forty nights of listening to elephants, crocodiles, zebras, and Mr. Noah snoring their heads off—and in waltzed that darling dove with an olive twig in its blessed little bill! Go on—whistle it again for her!"

But, this time, the song had no magic. It was the old, beloved tune which had once summoned her and had said, "Come, Susannah, I need you,"—but it wasn't coming from the lips of David Blake. The tail stopped in mid wag. The ears dropped. She slumped to the floor, put her head on her paws and closed her eyes.

"Drat it!" said Mrs. Noah. "Drat! Drat! *Drat*!"

"Maybe," suggested her youngest, "if you whistled it for her—"

"I'm just too discouraged to pucker," sighed his mother. "Well—tomorrow's another day and I may think of something. You run along and do your chores—and mind you change the water in that tin can with the tadpole named 'Prince' that came yesterday from Ashtabula, Ohio!"

Mrs. Noah walked morosely through the Ark and out

onto her front porch, which Joseph, a kindly man and an excellent carpenter, had made for her many years before as a birthday gift. It had trellises for her rambling roses and a good stout floor for her favorite rocker. To the left of it was her prized rock garden, which had been another birthday gift. This had come from Samson, mighty in strength, who had carefully selected each stone and had lugged it all the way from the far Vale of Valhalla. In spite of her uncertain temper and acid tongue, Mrs. Noah had many warm friends in the great Celestial City.

She rocked lugubriously to and fro—taking little notice of the many people who nightly roamed the Street of Miracles, hoping to come upon the unexpected and unbelievable around a twist or turning of its roundabout and exciting way.

"Good evening, Mrs. Noah," said a grave, low voice.

"Evening," that lady responded shortly. Then, recognizing the speaker as a neighbor who dwelt a few doors away, she allowed herself to become more cordial. "Good evening, dearie!" It always turned Mrs. Noah's stomach to utter this insipid endearment, but this dark and lovely young woman had a tongue-tying Egyptian name which she could neither pronounce nor remember.

"Been fishing again, dearie?" She raised her voice to reach the girl, who, with her basket of woven reeds, was being borne swiftly away by the crowd. "Any luck tonight?"

"Oh, yes, indeed!" The Egyptian's voice was merry in the distance. "Would you believe it—there were two—a boy and a girl!"

"Ah?" Mrs. Noah smiled. Think of that—a pair of newly-born babes for the House of the Pharaoh's Daughter on the

Street of Miracles. It was too bad and a shame that the tearful mothers of these little lost nurslings couldn't know that the mites had been saved by the same pair of gentle merciful hands which had rescued the infant, Moses, from the reeds by the river.

David came by, walking tall as Goliath—and Cap'n Cabe Tollivar, passing out handbills which advertised tomorrow night's show at the Magnolia Blossom Showboat on Bayou Creole at Fiddlers' Green—and Abel, the shepherd and son of Eve, in quest of a silver bell for his flock on the green, fertile Pastures of Eden—and rolly-polly Otto Schnitter, on his way to a shop to purchase sweets for the children who would be aboard his school bus on the morrow.

"Hello, Mrs. Noah."

The lady blinked her eyes and snapped herself from her reverie. The speaker was her good friend, Francis. He sat down on the top step of her porch, drew up his long legs and rested his chin on his bony knees.

"Evening, Francis."

"I had a few minutes—they're making extra space on my carrier for tonight's trip. There were a lot of small creatures who fell fast asleep today—and a number of large ones. An old, work-worn camel at a camp on the Gobi desert; a lame, year-battered llama in Peru; a foot-weary dancing bear at a traveling circus near Budapest... How's the dog?"

"What dog?"

"You know very well what dog. The one I brought you the other day. Her name is Susannah."

"Oh, that one." Mrs. Noah kicked with her feet and her rocker rolled back and forth like a skiff on an angry sea.

"You've brought me whole slews of dogs—I've got hundreds on my hands. How would a body know which animal you walked all the way up here to... Well, if you really want to know, that Susannah is driving me right out of my mind. I'm not worried, you understand—but it does fret me that I haven't found the key to her trouble."

"Well," said Francis, "I've been giving the matter quite a bit of thought. It's my belief that Susannah doesn't feel needed."

"Just what do you mean by that?" demanded Mrs. Noah.

"From puppyhood, she was trained to be the eyes of the blind. David Blake depended upon her to lead him safely and surely wherever he wished to go. She was indispensable. She was needed. Responsibility made her happy. Right now, she can be of no service to anyone—and therefore, she is miserable."

"Hmmmm," mused Mrs. Noah. "You know, you might have something." She rocked for a few moments in deep contemplation of this new idea. "Tell me this—those seeing-eye dogs—they wear a kind of special harness, don't they?"

"Yes," Francis nodded. "They do."

"I'll get one."

"Oh, Mrs. Noah!" he protested. "Where, in the Celestial City where such things aren't needed, would you ever find one?"

"Barnabas will have it. That place he calls 'The Impossible Shop,' right here on the Street of Miracles, has everything."

"But this thing is impossibly impossible!"

"No such thing!" retorted Mrs. Noah. "It's possibly possible! What about that carnival fellow who came up here and was just pining away with nothing to do—and they let

217

him put together his flea circus just around the corner from Angels' Aide? He was stuck for costumes for his hippity-hop cast—and he went to Barnabas! He got evening gowns, ballet dresses, and afternoon frocks! He even got flea bikinis in case he ever wanted to do a beach scene!"

"That, if I may point it out, was a most unusual circumstance—"

"This is an unusual circumstance! And if Barnabas can dress a flea, he can certainly dress a seeing-eye dog! I'll see him tomorrow. No—he'll still be open—I'll see him tonight!" Mrs. Noah rose to her feet. "Good evening, Francis." She clumped down the steps and started off up the winding Street of Miracles.

Since she was a longtime resident, the vagaries of the wandering Street of Miracles neither confused nor confounded her. She turned left seven times, right nine times, doubled back on her tracks five times and there it was—looking very unspick-and-unspan— "The Impossible Shop, Unlimited."

The interior of Barnabas' establishment resembled the untidy nest of a jackdaw whose acquisitive career had been long and fruitful. From floor to ceiling and from wall to wall, it was filled with cases, hampers, crates, sacks, trunks, boxes, chests, barrels, cabinets, casks, baskets, and bins.

"My dear Mrs. Noah!" Barnabas, after a busy day, had been resting on a keg marked "Pipettes and Poppets"—but he leaped to his feet as she entered the door. "This is a pleasant surprise and an honor! What can I do for you?"

"I would like a harness," said the lady. "A nice harness for a seeing-eye dog."

"Oh, my!" Barnabas pursed his lips. "That is a hard one."

"Have you got one?" demanded Mrs. Noah.

"Well, yes—somewhere—but just at the moment, I can't think where." He sighed and looked at his overstuffed storehouse. He turned back and his face brightened. "Perhaps—and I think this is an excellent suggestion— perhaps, for the time being, we could make a substitution. Now, here—this sea shell is an extraordinary piece of merchandise! If you hold it to your ear, you can hear again the conversation which took place on any day in your past!"

"I wouldn't be interested," said Mrs. Noah.

"Don't you think it would be exciting to recall one of those forty days on the Ark and hear again what Mr. Noah said?"

"No, I don't." The lady was emphatic. "Mr. Noah was never a brilliant conversationalist. In fact, in all the years we've been married, I don't remember that he's ever give out with a single word worth recounting."

"Oh—then how about this pin? Now, from all appearance, it is just a common pin—but on its head is engraved the earth's total knowledge of mathematics, astronomy, and physics!"

"Nope."

"This alarm clock, then! This, now, is really unusual and would please anyone! At night, when you go to bed, you set this dial for any year in your past. When you drop off to sleep, you'll dream all the beautiful events of that year!"

"I didn't come here for gewgaws or fripperies," said Mrs. Noah. "All I want is a seeing-eye dog harness. Is there one in stock?"

"Didn't I say I had one somewhere?" Barnabas asked plaintively. "But I have to look for it, Mrs. Noah! I may have to look the whole night! Why don't you come back tomorrow?"

"I'll wait," said the lady. She sat down on the pipettes and poppets keg and closed her eyes. "It's been a weary day—and if I should nap off, just give me a good nudge when you locate my harness."

The next morning, when the harness was buckled on Susannah, Mr. Noah said that he had never seen such a change in an animal in all his days on the Ark. Once again Susannah became the proud protector, watchful of eye and anxious to cope with any emergency.

"Don't she look just lovely?" laughed Mrs. Noah. "You know what I'm going to do now? I'm going to take her for a walk!"

"Wearing that harness?" asked her shocked husband.

"And why not, I'd like to know?"

"The neighbors will talk—that's why not!"

"Let them gabble all they want. If I want to be led about by a seeing-eye dog, that's my business!"

And off they went—and they had a fine time. She and Susannah went along Eden Way, out the Avenue of Adoration to Third Millennium Circle, over to the Avenue of Compassion, and back to the Ark.

However, their passage was not unnoticed. People did stop and stare in great astonishment. Some even followed. In fact, when they returned home to the Ark, it looked as though Mrs. Noah and Susannah were leading a parade. After the two had disappeared in the door, the people stood there, shaking heads, whispering, and click-clucking their tongues. The performance which they had just witnessed was a complete and unsolvable mystery, since everyone knew there was no blindness in the Celestial City.

That afternoon, Mrs. Noah and Susannah went shopping on Robemakers' Lane. That evening, they went to see a play on the Magnolia Blossom Showboat at Fiddlers' Green. The next afternoon, they attended a meeting of the sewing circle at Angels' Aide. That night, they walked together through the great Plaza of Eternity.

Later in the week, they chanced to come upon Otto Schnitter's big yellow school bus as it was about to roll earthward to pick up the daily flock of tots and toddlers. Susannah had been prideful of her ability to take David Blake aboard such a vehicle—and so she led Mrs. Noah up the steps and guided the lady to a seat.

They both enjoyed the trip. To Susannah, it was like the happytime Sunday excursion with David Blake. To Mrs. Noah, who hadn't seen the earth for quite a few centuries, it was most educational. It was amazing to observe how the inhabitants had changed things about. Some of the changes were good and many of them atrocious. On the return trip, the children made much of Susannah and Mrs. Noah had a nice gossip with Otto Schnitter.

But someone made a complaint. It couldn't have come from Peter at the great Gates because he has never been a trouble maker. Besides, he has a mush-soft spot in his old heart for Mrs. Noah. He proved this that time she brought the sickly monkey from the Ark and let it swing on the famous

Gates for exercise. Peter had turned his back and pretended to comb some non-existent snarls out of his white beard.

And, most certainly, the complaint was not made by Francis, Christopher, Barnabas, Samson, Joseph, David, Abel, or any other one of Mrs. Noah's good friends. Or by Lud, Angel of the Peace in the Plaza of Eternity. For all Lud cared, the lady could have galloped down the winding walks on a polka dot camel. Mrs. Noah was a fine woman and she should be allowed to be a bit eccentric.

Otto Schnitter guessed—and he may have been correct— that the complaint was made by Sheleph, keeper of star 482,764,283, the loneliest signal light station of the great celestial transport system. Shilly-shally Sheleph, he was called by some, and he led a hermit-like life on this far, isolated post. He was known for small acts of spite—but for these acts, he was really blameless. As a child, while playing on a street in Jerusalem, he had accidentally touched the robe of Judas of Kerioth.

The complaint, having been made, went from bureau to bureau and from department to department. In so doing, the complaint grew into an accusation. Scribes bent low over sheets of foolscap, their flying feathered pens inscribing the charge. Mrs. Noah, of the Ark, Number 10, Street of Miracles, was ordered to present herself for trial before the High Court of the Patriarch Prophets on Tuesday next.

She was accused of bearing false witness against a cardinal truth of the Celestial City: to wit, the fulfilled promise that all lame shall walk and all blind shall see. Mrs. Noah, her vision no less keen than anyone else within the Gates, had willfully, persistently, and arrogantly presented herself to the public view, on street, avenue, and conveyance, in the utterly false role of a poor, handicapped female, who was unable to go about without the help of a lead animal.

"The law!" There was bitter scorn in the voice of Dysmas, the thief, who had been a good friend of the Proprietor's Son since a day on Calvary. "The law hasn't changed one nose-poking bit since Pilate's time!"

"If they banish her," moaned Francis, "what will become of the Ark? Noah and the boys are all right—but without Mrs. Noah to crack her tongue over their backs—!"

"A fine woman—persecuted by bookish midges!" growled the mighty Samson. "If we were on earth and I was a few thousand years younger, I'd give that High Court building a good shove!"

It was unnecessary for the dignitaries of the High Court of the Patriarch Prophets to bend their august knees and put their honorable ears to the ground to hear what was being said the length and breadth of the Celestial City. One by one, they disqualified themselves for a variety of reasons. Some owned pets which had come by way of the Ark. Others claimed cousinship, a million or so times removed. Several said that they could never deliver an impartial verdict because they had enjoyed Mrs. Noah's strawberry tarts at a church supper.

Solomon, the wise son of David, was asked to preside—and after deep and agonizing thought and a prayer to the Proprietor to give him wisdom beyond wisdom, he left his house in the Down of Promise and came to Eden Way, to ascend the bench of the High Court of the Patriarch Prophets.

It was a long and tedious trial. The defense called 9,783

witnesses—and each one eagerly attested Mrs. Noah's piety, virtue, integrity, honor, generosity, and benevolence.

The prosecution, browbeating the same 9,783 testifiers, obtained the reluctant admission that Mrs. Noah was also obstinate, ruthless, antagonistic, contrary, tyrannical, abusive, and cantankerous.

In its summation, the prosecution said:

"We are not here, O Solomon, to judge Mrs. Noah's character! Be she a veritable pearl of womankind or a hateful harridan is not germane to this trial! The question is—the *only* question is—*did she or did she not go about this city with a seeing-eye dog?* I call your attention to the defendant, Mrs. Noah, at this very moment! She sits over there—with the dog, Susannah, beside her—and she brazenly—nay, *contemptuously*—holds fast to that harness which proclaims her sightless! 'False witness!' I cry. There is no such affliction in the Celestial City! O Solomon—O wise and honored Solomon—I demand a conviction!"

"I will think on it," said Solomon. "The court is adjourned until after the Sabbath."

When the church bells called, Solomon was walking in his garden at the Down of Promise. He had much to think about and the Proprietor would understand and condone his absence.

The verdict. What should the verdict be? Mrs. Noah was guilty of the charge beyond a whisper of a doubt. Her intentions were good—but law was black on white and shouldn't be faded to gray by intentions.

Still, she was such a good woman. However, a bad act by

a good woman didn't make it a good bad act.

Why did I ever consent to sit in judgment, he thought. *I am an old ox who should have remained in his stall munching on the harvest of past glory, when I exceeded all the kings of the earth for riches and wisdom.*

In the old days—ah, the old days!—when the queen of Sheba journeyed to Jerusalem to observe my sagacity—I could have disposed of this case before one could say, "Hazor, Megiddo, and Gezer."

The prosecution had proven its case. As judge, he would, on the morrow, have to say that Mrs. Noah was guilty as charged. Shaking his head and sighing deeply, Solomon went in to his Sabbath dinner.

That night, as the hours passed, he lay sleepless. Finally, when a distant watch angel called, "Three o'clock! Three o'clock on a fine, clear, celestial evening—and all's well!," he arose from his rumpled bed, put on a robe and went down into his garden.

It was bathed in the bright light of the Proprietor's many moons. Solomon walked slowly down the path which was bordered by rose bushes of every color. They rose higher than his head—sturdy of branch, green of leaf, and heavy with bloom.

His slow footsteps came to a halt. He looked down at a scraggly bit of growth that rose no more than twelve inches above the soil. Its thorns were cruel. Its leaves were limp and few. It bore one wilted blossom.

His wives had often said that it should be pulled up because it spoiled the appearance of the whole garden. Solomon had indignantly refused to destroy it. With care, he had stoutly stated, it would grow round and tall and green and would deck itself in a lovely profusion of flowers which would be unequaled, anywhere in the entire city, in size and perfume.

Day after day, he had given this dwarfed bush his personal care. It puzzled him that his wives couldn't see what he could see so clearly—the unparalleled beauty which was sleeping in its obdurate roots.

Solomon bent and gently touched a drooping leaf. A thought, sharp as a rose thorn, then pricked his mind and, from the wound, the truth came welling out like blood from a pierced finger. He straightened and smote his brow with a clenched fist.

"Why, that's it!" he murmured. "And it's so simple that Balaam's donkey would have understood it with but a tail-flick of thought. O Solomon—Solomon! How dull and stupid you have become! A dolt—a witless dolt—a numskull! Why, if he were caught in a storm old fuzzy-brained Solomon wouldn't have sense enough to crawl in out of the rain!"

The next day, it seemed as though the entire Celestial City had come to hear the judgment of Solomon. The courtroom of the Patriarch Prophets and all the corridors of the great building were crammed with people. Outside, Eden Way and the Plaza of Eternity were a sea of faces. Sukie, the red-haired cherub from Angels' Aide, had done some climbing and was seated in the topmost pan of the Scale of Justice. In spite of a grandmother's pleading, she refused to descend—and explained that from down below, her pet turtle Picklepuss wouldn't be able to see and hear Solomon.

Samson had brought Mrs. Noah's rocker to the courtroom

*Mrs. Noah and Susannah listen to testimony in
wise old Solomon's courtroom.*

and the accused was rocking herself slowly to and fro. She had replaced the singed posies in her summer-garden-after-a-cloudburst hat and she appeared very respectable and matronly. Susannah, wearing her seeing-eye harness, sat beside Mrs. Noah with five inches of tongue hanging out in a pleased grin. It had been a happy responsibility to guide Mrs. Noah through the crowd to this busy and exciting place.

"Silence! Silence in the courtroom!" a voice cried, snuffing the roar of the crowd as though it were a candle. Solomon lifted his head and spoke:

"For these many years, I have believed—as all of us have sincerely believed—that there is no blindness in our Celestial City.

"Is this really and absolutely so?

"If it is so, why do the children, who come to us on Otto Schnitter's school bus, describe him as a tall, stalwart figure of a man, with a lullaby voice—when, in reality, Mr. Schnitter is quite short, very fat and if he sang a lullaby, he might be mistaken for a bullfrog?

"Have you ever been bewildered when talking with Angela Barnworth, at Canaan Common? She has proudly told all of us that her Old Cat is a veritable tomcat Adonis. You and I cannot see this beauty. To us, he is a plain, ordinary stray, born and bred in an earthly alley.

"At Fiddlers' Green, each sailor believes that his ship is superior to any other ship in that whole, heavenlocked harbor. At Happy Hunting Ground, each brave will boast that his fine teepee is the best. At Trails' End, each covered wagon is a palace on wheels to its owner when he looks down his nose at other vehicles. But ships, teepees, or wagons—

they appear much the same to us.

"Last evening, in my garden, I discovered that I, too, have this affliction. I looked at a small rose bush and saw beauty— and yet the seven hundred sharp-eyed women of my house have scorned it as ugly. But seven hundred against one does not prove that what I saw is false. To me, it is beautiful because I have cherished and loved it.

"On earth, there is blindness of both the eye and the heart. In the Celestial City, all eyes can see but the heart remains sightless when examining persons or objects of its affection.

"In the opinion of this court, a blindfolded mole has greater vision than Mrs. Noah. To relieve the unhappiness or discontent of any one of her charges, her heart cannot see anything strange, bizarre, or outlandish in the most incredible act she may do in loving blindness.

"She is stone-blind to scorn.

"She is stark-blind to ridicule.

"She is pure-blind to any and all consequences.

"Such being so, I rule for the defendant, Mrs. Noah—and I censure the prosecution for its shameful persecution of a lady so sorely afflicted.

"Case dismissed and court adjourned."

Almost any day now, one of the great transports will burst through the bank of morning mist, carrying its passengers to the foot of the famous Stairs. In Peter's book, one of them will be listed as "Blake, David."

Francis, with a stray canary or parakeet feather in his tousled hair, will meet him at the Gates. Together, they will hurry across the Plaza of Eternity by the short-cut known only to Francis—and which saves a full two minutes.

Upon entering the wonderful old Ark on the Street of Miracles, David will find himself engulfed in a bedlam of barks, squeaks, chirps, meows, grunts, and birdsongs. It will always be thus with the appearance of any newcomer. The separation may have been for a week, a year, or a decade, but each furry or feathery guest will always firmly believe that this footfall is bringing the hand and voice it remembers.

Susannah, when she sees David, will moan and howl and whimper and come near to turning herself inside out in pure ecstasy. When he holds her head in his hands—seeing her for the first time in all the years they have shared—her heart, for one dreadful moment, will stop. She will realize that David will have no further need for her eyes. Her eyes will then plead— "Now that I am useless, will you forsake me?"

David will whistle "O Susannah"—and she will live again. Without the harness, they will leave the Ark and walk down the Street of Miracles—and for the first time, David will lead and Susannah will follow.

"Good-bye!" Mrs. Noah will go out on her porch to see them off. "Good-bye, now!"

She will watch them out of sight—and then she will re-enter the Ark and pick up the discarded seeing-eye harness.

"I won't be wanting this anymore," she will say to Mr. Noah. "You can put it away somewhere."

"Yes, Mother."

"I certainly am real glad to get rid of that Susannah. It'll be a treat to go out by myself and not have to think about her. Yes, sir—a real treat."

All that day, Mrs. Noah's temper will be uncertain and her three sons will try to keep out of her way.

Supper will be a silent affair.

Late that night, after checking snores to be sure the boys and her husband are fast asleep, she will come down the old stairs and stand by the mat which belonged to Susannah. Standing there, she will wipe her eyes and blow her nose and make a soggy mess of a handkerchief.

For those who believe Mrs. Noah to be obstinate, contrary and cantankerous, this will be a miracle as big as a hippopotamus.

If Mrs. Noah, grieving for some pet, wept for forty days and forty nights and put the old Ark afloat, it would be a very small miracle.

Very small.

Ladybug size.

For those who truly understand the blindness of love, it will be no miracle at all.